DEAD ON ARRIVAL

LANTERN BEACH P.D., BOOK 4

CHRISTY BARRITT

Squeaky Clean Mysteries:
   #1 Hazardous Duty
   #2 Suspicious Minds
   #2.5 It Came Upon a Midnight Crime (novella)
   #3 Organized Grime
   #4 Dirty Deeds
   #5 The Scum of All Fears
   #6 To Love, Honor and Perish
   #7 Mucky Streak
   #8 Foul Play
   #9 Broom & Gloom
   #10 Dust and Obey
   #11 Thrill Squeaker
   #11.5 Swept Away (novella)
   #12 Cunning Attractions

#13 Cold Case: Clean Getaway

#14 Cold Case: Clean Sweep

While You Were Sweeping, A Riley Thomas Spinoff

The Sierra Files:

#1 Pounced

#2 Hunted

#3 Pranced

#4 Rattled

#5 Caged (coming soon)

The Gabby St. Claire Diaries (a Tween Mystery series):

The Curtain Call Caper

The Disappearing Dog Dilemma

The Bungled Bike Burglaries

The Worst Detective Ever

#1 Ready to Fumble

#2 Reign of Error

#3 Safety in Blunders

#4 Join the Flub

#5 Blooper Freak

#6 Flaw Abiding Citizen

#7 Gaffe Out Loud

#8 Joke and Dagger (coming soon)

Raven Remington
Relentless 1
Relentless 2 (coming soon)

Holly Anna Paladin Mysteries:
#1 Random Acts of Murder
#2 Random Acts of Deceit
#2.5 Random Acts of Scrooge
#3 Random Acts of Malice
#4 Random Acts of Greed
#5 Random Acts of Fraud
#6 Random Acts of Outrage
#7 Random Acts of Iniquity (coming soon)

Lantern Beach Mysteries
#1 Hidden Currents
#2 Flood Watch
#3 Storm Surge
#4 Dangerous Waters
#5 Perilous Riptide
#6 Deadly Undertow

Lantern Beach Romantic Suspense
Tides of Deception

Shadow of Intrigue

Storm of Doubt

Lantern Beach P.D.

On the Lookout

Attempt to Locate

First Degree Murder

Dead on Arrival

Plan of Action (coming in May)

Carolina Moon Series

Home Before Dark

Gone By Dark

Wait Until Dark

Light the Dark

Taken By Dark

Suburban Sleuth Mysteries:

Death of the Couch Potato's Wife

Fog Lake Suspense:

Edge of Peril

Margin of Error (coming soon)

Cape Thomas Series:

Dubiosity

Disillusioned

Distorted

Standalone Romantic Mystery:

The Good Girl

Suspense:

Imperfect

The Wrecking

Standalone Romantic-Suspense:

Keeping Guard

The Last Target

Race Against Time

Ricochet

Key Witness

Lifeline

High-Stakes Holiday Reunion

Desperate Measures

Hidden Agenda

Mountain Hideaway

Dark Harbor

Shadow of Suspicion

The Baby Assignment

The Cradle Conspiracy (coming soon)

Nonfiction:

Characters in the Kitchen

Changed: True Stories of Finding God through Christian Music (out of print)

The Novel in Me: The Beginner's Guide to Writing and Publishing a Novel (out of print)

CHAPTER ONE

MORIAH GILEAD LACED her fingers with her husband's as they walked through the crowd, shaking hands and offering words of affirmation. Everyone around them adored this man—and for good reason.

Anthony Gilead was amazing.

The two of them had arrived back from their honeymoon only one day ago. Her new husband had taken her to a secluded cabin in the mountains of North Carolina. They hadn't left the location all week.

Her cheeks flushed at the thought.

They continued to walk past the residents of Gilead's Cove and ended their trek with Gilead taking the small stage at the front of the room.

Today was the big day—election day here on the island of Lantern Beach.

Up until three days ago, Moriah had no idea Gilead was even running for mayor.

A lump formed in her throat at the memory.

She thought Gilead would have mentioned that fact to her earlier. But he must have had good reason not to. Moriah had to stop being so quick to judge.

She remained by the wooden steps leading to the aged stage, staying to the side of the crowd and holding her hands in front of her like a good, supportive wife. A *submissive* wife. Gilead had had many conversations with her about this new role she'd taken on and what it meant.

"Residents of Gilead's Cove and followers of the Cause," Gilead started, gripping the podium as his engaged expression latched onto anyone listening. "It's great to be back with you."

Everyone cheered.

Today's event was a change from the normal morning pep session Gilead led. Something about him getting married, going away, and running for mayor seemed to ignite a new excitement in his followers.

"Today is going to be a good day." He flashed a bright smile.

More cheers.

Gilead obviously felt confident he was going to win this election. And why shouldn't he? The man was smart and charming. He had a way about him that made people want to do things for him. Only great leaders possessed that trait and could use it so masterfully.

"So, how was your honeymoon?" someone whispered.

Moriah glanced over and saw Ruth had sidled up beside her. The woman had been Moriah's mentor when she'd first arrived here at the Cove. The two of them hadn't spoken since Moriah had returned from her trip, and Moriah had no desire to talk to the woman about anything personal now.

Though it *would* be nice to talk to *someone* about personal things. To whisper secrets and to share the highs and lows of her new marriage. Maybe even someone Moriah could ask advice from without fear of being reprimanded and judged.

Instead, Moriah offered a tight smile at the quiet question. "It was wonderful."

Ruth quirked a shaggy eyebrow as she studied Moriah's face. "Glad to hear that."

Moriah nibbled on the inside of her cheek. If she were talking to a trusted friend right now, she might tell the truth. Might share that her honeymoon hadn't been anything like she'd imagined.

In her mind, the trip would be full of tender moments where she and Gilead bonded together as husband and wife. After all, they still had so much to learn about each other. Their courtship had been short and hurried, to say the least.

Instead of tender moments, the whole experience had felt like an exercise in . . . greed and insatiability.

Moriah swallowed hard. She would never make that admission aloud. Besides, no one would believe her. Everyone thought Gilead was God. That he was perfect. Blameless. Righteous.

Her expectations for their trip had simply been unrealistic. Still, she ran a hand over her lips, wishing she could erase the feel of her husband's mouth against hers.

What had once seemed forbidden and romantic now caused nausea to rise in her.

She would adjust. Eventually, she'd tell Gilead her concerns over their relationship. Certainly, something between them would change when she shared with him. He'd understand that Moriah needed more of a personal connection and that otherwise she simply felt like a cheap escort.

"Why do you look pale?" Ruth's eyes bore into Moriah.

Moriah tensed at the question. "I don't look pale."

"Don't tell me you don't look pale. I'm looking right at you."

Moriah shrugged, unwilling to take the bait. "It's a big day. That's all."

As Gilead continued to captivate everyone in the room, Ruth's attention remained on Moriah. "We're all headed into town to vote later. You too?"

"I haven't registered to vote in Lantern Beach, and I didn't know—" Moriah stopped herself before she said too much.

"You didn't know your husband was running for mayor?" Was that delight in Ruth's voice? Was the woman looking for cracks in their marriage so she could exploit them? Or so she could feel better about herself and her own problems?

The last thing Moriah wanted was anyone feeling sorry for her—or that they had the upper hand.

"We didn't have much time to talk before we got married." Moriah kept her voice placid and professional. "It's not a big deal."

Ruth leaned closer to be heard over Gilead. "I'd say it was. If your husband wins this election, your life is going to look different. He's going to have other responsibilities besides Gilead's Cove. Other priorities besides you."

Something ached inside Moriah at Ruth's words, but she raised her shoulders, desperate not to show her doubts. "I trust my husband, but I'm still not sure why he wants this."

"Power, my dear. Power."

Just as Ruth said the words, the doors to the Meeting Place opened. A group of people Moriah had never seen before flooded inside.

She sucked in a quick, surprised breath. "What . . . ?"

"We're busing them in," Ruth whispered. "Isn't it wonderful?"

Moriah's hand clutched the fabric of her dress near her neck. "Busing them in from where?"

"Everywhere. The scouts have begun recruiting. We're expecting another busload later, and we'll probably get twenty or thirty more people every week from here on out. We need to expand. But first we need the proper permits."

Realization hit Moriah. Permits? Was that really why Gilead was interested in taking over Lantern Beach? So he could do what he wanted when he wanted how he wanted?

That sounded like her husband—in more than one way.

Moriah tried to push aside her anxiety, but it wouldn't subside.

Something bad was going to happen here on this island.

Moriah could feel it in her gut. And she had no choice but to trust her husband. Otherwise, she'd face the wrath of the Council . . . wrath that Gilead had told her included punishments she couldn't even imagine suffering.

Her chance at a new life was suddenly feeling like a new chance at retribution against her for all the mistakes she'd made in her past.

Why had she ever thought coming here was a good idea?

CHAPTER TWO

AS A CHILLY BREEZE swept across the shore and over the sand dune that stood guard in front of her cottage, Cassidy Chambers pulled her blanket closer around her shoulders.

She stood in her favorite place—the screened-in porch that faced the ocean. As her husband, Ty, stepped up behind her, she melted into him and let herself get lost for a moment in the spicy scent of his cologne. With a cup of coffee in hand, their dog, Kujo, at her feet, and the morning sun shining just above the horizon, the day promised to be a good one.

She could use a good day. In her short tenure as police chief, too many things here on Lantern Beach had gone wrong. Too many crimes. Conspiracies. Threats.

Stress had accumulated in Cassidy, evidenced by shoulders that were constantly tight, a body that continually craved caffeine, and a distant headache that frequently wanted to pulse at her temples.

"Things are going to turn around," Ty murmured in Cassidy's ear, as if sensing her heavy thoughts.

"I know." Cassidy rested her free hand on top of her husband's, treasuring the fact that he was her safe place. Always. "I'll just be happy to have this election over with."

Today the town would elect their new mayor. Three people were in the running: current mayor Mike Tomlinson, former police chief Mac MacArthur, and newcomer Anthony Gilead.

"You don't really think Anthony Gilead is going to win, do you?" Ty seemed to read her thoughts yet again.

Cassidy caught her bottom lip and nibbled on it as she frowned. "I want to say no. I really do. But I've seen crazier things happen before, so I never say never."

"Yeah, I get that."

She drew in a deep breath, trying to wrap her mind around everything that would be transpiring today. Though she'd been a detective in Seattle, this would be her first small-town election. It was proving to be more stressful than she ever imagined.

"We have one voting site here on the island," Cassidy said, voicing her thoughts aloud as she raised her coffee mug and continued to stare out over the water. "My crew and I will be busy all day monitoring the location. We don't anticipate any trouble but . . . we are on Lantern Beach."

"Plus, there are county officials who will be monitoring the location for election fraud. Everything will be okay, Cass."

"You think?" She wished she felt as confident, wished that statement was as certain as the smell of salty air present each morning.

"I do. And tonight we will be celebrating Mac's win. He's going to make a great mayor." Mac wasn't only the town's retired police chief, he was also their good friend.

"He will. He deserves this position. That's for sure." The ocean mesmerized her as it lapped the shore in wave after wave. The constants in her life were what reassured her—not only the water, but also God, Ty, and her circle of friends.

Ever since Cassidy had received some text messages threatening to reveal her past identity, her peace of mind had scattered like papers in the wind. Someone knew who she really was, and that put her —as well as everyone she cared about—in danger. Looking over her shoulder all the time was no way to live, yet it seemed to be a permanent reality for Cassidy.

"That was some party we had for Mac last night." Ty's chin dipped down and rested near her neck.

Cassidy took another sip of her coffee. "I wish I could have stayed. I'm still not sure why someone would try to steal a car on an island. As soon as they try to leave on the ferry, they're going to be caught."

"No one ever said criminals were smart."

"I can't argue with that. But I heard Lisa really hit it out of the park with her 'Mac-themed' food and drinks." Cassidy had only stopped by for a few minutes before she'd been called out to work. Though she hated to miss the party, it was her turn to be on evening duty.

"Mac and cheese with bacon, fast food knockoff Big Macs, Mac Daddy Sliders with french fries, fried mac-and-cheese balls," Ty said. "Lisa always goes above and beyond."

"Yes, she does." Their friend Lisa Dillinger had just gotten back from her honeymoon in time to host the event at her restaurant. The turnout had been great.

Cassidy would guess, based on what she'd briefly seen and heard, that nearly two hundred people had shown up at some point. Considering there were only six hundred locals on the island, Cassidy thought those numbers were outstanding.

Now, Cassidy hoped the turnout at the polls today would reflect all the campaigning that had been done and the qualifications Mac would bring to the office.

Cassidy's cell phone rang from its position on the railing in front of her.

She sighed and stared at it a moment, tempted to pretend she didn't hear it.

Of course she couldn't do that. Instead, she grabbed the device and answered, knowing all too well that early morning phone calls were never good. "Chief Chambers."

"Cassidy, it's Doc Clemson. We have a situation I thought you'd want to know about."

She tensed when she heard his serious tone. "What's going on?"

"We've had about twenty, twenty-five people come to the clinic this morning with food poisoning."

"Food poisoning?" She glanced at Ty, and he raised his eyebrows.

"Unfortunately, one of the patients was dead on arrival. I guess the food poisoning, when mixed with his already weakened immune system, was too much for his body to handle."

"Someone died? That's awful. I'm really sorry to

hear that." She stepped away from Ty, dreading where this conversation might go. As Cassidy looked back at him, she saw his eyes were fastened on hers, curiosity seeping from their depths.

"Cassidy, there's one thing that everyone here has in common."

She swallowed hard before asking, "What's that?"

"Everyone here was at Lisa's last night."

———

CASSIDY RELUCTANTLY LEFT Ty and Kujo and headed for the clinic. Ty had been kind enough to pour her coffee into a travel mug, allowing her to finish it on the short drive. She had to talk to Clemson in person and figure out what was going on here in Lantern Beach. Since someone had died, this was officially a police matter.

But a bad feeling rose in her gut.

Whatever had happened, it didn't sound good. Not at all. But she needed more information before proceeding.

Cassidy nodded hello to the weary-looking nurse behind the front desk. Around her, the small clinic looked like a scene from a disaster movie. People were on beds in the hallway, holding their stomachs.

The waiting room was packed. A putrid stench hung in the air.

She started toward Clemson's office, but thought twice about it. With all these people here, there was no way the doctor was doing paperwork right now. Instead, Cassidy scanned the rooms as she passed. At the second from the last room, Clemson stepped out just as she walked up.

The sixty-something man looked tired, like he'd been up all night. He probably had.

"Cassidy, you made it." He stopped and offered a weary smile as he slid a file into a pocket attached to the door. "I could use a quick break. Come on into my office."

She followed him to the end of the hallway and into his office. After shutting the door, he took a seat behind his desk and pushed his glasses higher on his nose. A frown dug into his wrinkled face.

"Have a seat." He nodded at the padded brown chair in front of him.

Cassidy sat and stared at the island's only doctor and, by default, the town's esteemed medical examiner. "As you can imagine, I'm anxious to hear more. Are you certain it's food poisoning and not the stomach flu?"

Clemson let out a long breath. "Certain? No. Nearly certain? Yes. We'll send samples to the lab, of course. But the fact that everyone who is ill ate at Lisa's last night confirms to me that this isn't just a virus."

"You said one person died?" The words burned in Cassidy's throat. She hated to even think about it, to imagine the family who was grieving now.

"That's correct. Morty Simpson. He had lupus. His body just couldn't handle everything."

Morty Simpson? Cassidy had met the man once. He was a bit reclusive, and some in town even called him backward. He was single, and he had one adult son named Frankie. If Cassidy remembered correctly, Morty worked as a boat captain and did charter tours from the island.

"How is everyone else doing?" Cassidy asked.

Clemson shoved some files in front of him aside and frowned. "Well, ten more people have been admitted since I called you. Fever. Headache. Chills. Vomiting. It's not a pretty scene out there, and we're running out of room. We may have to call in backup to help because we're not staffed to handle this many sick people."

Cassidy shook her head, feeling frustration well inside her. "But I know Lisa. She's too responsible to let something like this happen."

He frowned again. "It can happen even to the best. Maybe it wasn't Lisa at all. Maybe it was one of the foods she purchased. Maybe there needs to be a recall on some produce or seafood."

"Does everyone else seem okay? No one else is on death's door or anything?" Cassidy prayed that wasn't the case, that this outbreak would subside instead of worsening.

"Not that I know of. Let's hope not."

"What's the next step?" She was the police chief and needed to think like a cop instead of a friend right now. But what was the protocol for something like this? She had no experience in dealing with massive food-poisoning outbreaks.

"I'll have to call the Department of Health. They'll do an investigation. We need to find the source of this before other people become ill."

That made sense.

Cassidy shifted, knowing that the events about to be set in motion would turn her friend's life upside down. She cleared her throat before asking, "Clemson, have you told Lisa yet?"

He shook his head, the action heavy and burdened. Almost everyone in Lantern Beach loved Lisa and wanted only the best for her. "No, I haven't been able to bring myself to do it."

Cassidy stood. "I will."

She didn't want to be the one to break the news. Didn't want to see the joy slip from her friend's eyes.

Lisa had looked so happy earlier since returning from her honeymoon. She'd delighted in hosting Mac's party at The Crazy Chefette. She'd been anticipating opening full-time for the season this weekend.

And now this.

"You sure?" Clemson asked.

Cassidy nodded. "Yeah, I'm sure. It needs to come from a friend. Plus, I'm going to have to get involved. Someone died. This is much bigger than mere food poisoning at this point. This will shut Lisa's restaurant down. If people think negligence is involved, it could even lead to some civil cases. It's hard to say right now. But it will probably get uglier before it gets better."

"I'll be praying for everyone involved."

Cassidy stood. "Thank you. This town is going to need it."

CHAPTER THREE

CASSIDY HESITATED before knocking on the back door to Lisa's place. Lisa and her husband, Braden, lived in the apartment upstairs above The Crazy Chefette. The restaurant was closed today, still on the off-season schedule.

As Cassidy waited, she enjoyed the balmy sunshine that warmed her shoulders. She sucked in a deep breath, feeling a fleeting moment of refreshment. Summertime was getting close. She could almost smell it.

And, as much as she didn't want to admit it, Cassidy almost looked forward to tourist season. It would bring about a different set of problems here on the island: arguments at rental properties, stolen goods from cars left unlocked—mostly by tourists— and lots of speeding tickets.

Those things, while not good, seemed much better than the crimes that had happened on the island these past few months. Things were supposed to slow down here in the cold weather with everyone huddling inside, enacting the island's version of hibernation.

A moment later, a sleepy-eyed Lisa padded down the stairs—Cassidy could see her through the window—and opened the back door.

Lisa blinked the sleep out of her eyes, as if still trying to wake up. "Cassidy. What brings you here so early?"

Dread pooled in Cassidy's stomach. Her friend had no idea her world was about to be rocked. No idea.

"Can we talk a second?" Cassidy asked.

"Of course. Come on in. I'd offer you coffee, but I don't have any made yet. I think I'm still tired from going to Cancun and then staying up late after the party."

Cassidy closed the door behind her, tension knotting the muscles in her back. "Don't worry about it. I take it you haven't talked to anyone this morning."

Certainly her friend wouldn't be this perky if she'd heard the news.

Lisa pulled her long, blonde hair back into a

sloppy ponytail. "No, I was exhausted after the party yesterday. I hate going to bed with a dirty kitchen, so I had to clean up. Braden likes to make fun of me about it."

More than anything, Cassidy wanted to smile and chat with her friend about her new marriage and island scuttlebutt. That wasn't a possibility right now, though.

"Lisa, you might need to sit down."

The light left her friend's eyes, replaced by confusion. "Sit down? Is something wrong?"

Cassidy pressed her lips together before saying, "You really should sit down first."

Wide-eyed, Lisa backed up and lowered herself onto one of the wooden steps that led up to her apartment. Before Cassidy could launch into her bad news, Braden lumbered down the stairs, muttered good morning, and sat beside his wife, lacing his fingers with hers.

"I wish I was here for a friendly chat," Cassidy started, each word requiring extra effort. "But, unfortunately, I'm here in an official capacity."

"Is something wrong? Is it Serena?" As Lisa frantically asked the question, Braden slipped his arm around her shoulder. Concern furrowed his brow.

Cassidy shook her head. Their friend Serena had

—against everyone's wishes—joined Gilead's Cove. The only way to get her out was if Serena left by her own free will, and she didn't appear willing to do that right now. They'd all been burdened by Serena's decision and prayed for her extensively.

Cassidy rubbed her hand across the stiff material of her police uniform, her palms clammy. "No, it's not Serena. It's about the party you had here for Mac last night."

Lisa's eyes narrowed. "What about it? I don't understand."

Cassidy swallowed hard, knowing that what she said next would feel like a slap in the face to her friend. There was no way she could dampen the effect of her words. They were going to hurt. "Lisa, almost forty people have come down with what appears to be food poisoning."

Her friend's face paled. "What? No . . . that's terrible."

Cassidy nodded, unable to shake her hesitation to reveal the truth to her friend. "And they all ate here."

Lisa's hand covered her mouth, which had rounded into an O of horror as Braden pulled her closer. "How is that even possible? You know I can be a neat freak. And I'm very particular—"

"I know you are," Cassidy interrupted. "But it gets worse."

"How can it possibly get worse than that?" Lisa's eyes were almost childlike as she stared at her.

Cassidy lifted up a prayer. "Lisa, someone died. We have no choice but to turn this over to the Department of Health. They'll have to do a full investigation. I'm so sorry. But you're going to have to delay your seasonal grand opening."

———

TY HIT his brakes at the end of the lane leading from his cottage, his vintage Chevy truck coming to a smooth stop. He watched as an old, beat-up school bus bumped past, headed toward the south end of the island.

"Where in the world did that bus come from?" he muttered, rubbing Kujo's back. His dog sat beside him, head—and tongue—hanging out the partially opened window of the passenger's seat.

The school system in town had yellow buses, and this one had been painted a light blue that had long since faded. The vehicle appeared to be loaded with people, and piles of baggage filled the back windows.

Ty sucked in a breath as a new thought slammed into his mind.

Had the bus been headed to . . . Gilead's Cove?

No. Ty shook his head. The thought was crazy.

Yet the possibility wouldn't leave his mind. That end destination was the only thing that made sense to him. Just a few places were located beyond Ty's cottage at this end of the island. Directly after his house, the landscape became wetlands then cut back into a narrow tip. The community church was there, along with a few houses, and farther down, on the sound side, was a place called Gilead's Cove.

On a whim, Ty turned the wheel of his truck and followed at an unassuming distance behind the oversized vehicle.

He slowed when he saw it pull through the gate into the compound known as Gilead's Cove.

A sickly feeling trickled in his gut. Even Kujo must have sensed the sentiment because he pulled his head back inside the window and licked Ty's hand as it rested on the gear shift.

Anthony Gilead must be bringing in new recruits.

Worst-case scenarios imploded in Ty's head.

The group was growing. They'd already bought up several other properties here on the island—properties besides the old RV park, where the majority of the people in the organization were housed. Just what was Anthony Gilead planning?

Whatever it was, it was big, and everyone on the island should be frightened.

As Ty watched the bus disappear from sight, his

phone rang. Cassidy gave him an update on the situation at Lisa's. His stomach clenched tighter at the news.

"This is bad, Cassidy." He still stared at the gated entrance to the compound, at the dust that the bus had stirred up as it turned onto the dusty gravel road. "Really bad."

"I know," Cassidy said. "How are you feeling? You ate at the party last night. I didn't since I was on duty, which just might have been a blessing in disguise."

"I'm okay. Since I'm trying to eat a high-protein diet right now, I only had some Mac Daddy Wings."

"That's all?"

He frowned. "Okay, so I may have snitched a bacon-wrapped jalapeno—I couldn't resist."

"Where's that Navy SEAL self-control you're known for?"

"Oh, it was there. Believe me. I could have filled my plate five times with all the food Lisa had prepared. Everything looked and smelled tasty."

In fact, Ty had gained five pounds since he'd gotten married, which was one of the reasons he'd decided to watch what he ate and to up his workouts. He wasn't quite ready to give into the weight gain associated with being happily married.

Cassidy, on the other hand, had probably lost ten

pounds over the past few weeks. The woman didn't have that much weight to lose, but he could tell the stress of everything was getting to her.

"I'm sure it did," Cassidy said. "And, just for the record, I love you, even with five extra pounds."

"And that's one more reason why you're amazing. But enough sweet talk for now. I've got to know—what happens next?" Lisa had to be beside herself. Ty lifted up a quick prayer for her sanity.

The playfulness left Cassidy's voice. "Inspectors from the Department of Health just arrived. They'll search the place and try to find the source of the outbreak. Meanwhile, the samples Clemson took have been fast-tracked. We should know something soon."

"I have other bad news," Ty said as he turned his truck around and headed toward the other end of the island. "I just saw a bus full of people pull into Gilead's Cove."

"What?" Cassidy's voice crept higher with tension. "You think it was full of new members?"

"That's my guess."

Cassidy paused before saying, "You don't think they're bringing people in for the election, do you?"

"I can't imagine that's the case." Despite that, the idea bothered Ty on more than one level. Gilead was slick. But was he slick enough to organize something like that? Ty wanted to say no, but he couldn't do so with confidence. "I mean, you have to be a resident here in Lantern Beach for at least thirty days in order to vote."

"I have a bad feeling, Ty. Anthony Gilead is a smart man. He may have figured out a way to bend the rules here."

Ty's thoughts echoed hers. She just hadn't wanted to voice the ideas aloud. "I know. What now?"

"Now, I need to go check on the voting site and make sure there's no trouble. Did you cast your ballot yet?"

"I was just on my way to do that when I saw the bus."

"After I make sure things are running smoothly, I may need to pay Gilead's Cove a visit. After all, I never talked to Moriah about her role in the incident last week where those men tried to kill me. I assume since Gilead is back in town that she is also."

A surge of protectiveness rose in him. "When you go, I want to go with you."

"I figured you'd say that. I'll give you a call before I head out there. Is that going to mess up your plans for work today? I know your next retreat starts soon."

"No, everything is set, and the new guests should

be arriving in three days. I have a few things to do before then, but they can wait."

"Perfect. I'll talk to you soon."

But as Ty ended the call, a bad feeling gurgled in his gut. Just what was going on here in Lantern Beach? And how were they going to stop it?

CHAPTER FOUR

CASSIDY CAST HER VOTE, fed her ballot into a machine, and then stepped back to the corner of this multi-purpose room in Lantern Beach's only school. With the island's small population, grades K-12 were all taught here in this one building.

Though it had been years since Cassidy had been in elementary school, the smell of cafeteria food lingered in the air and brought a wash of memories: greasy but limp french fries, chicken sandwiches on stale bread, unwanted applesauce spooned out onto a square section of a plastic tray.

The voting stations were set up in what was affectionately known as the gymnatorium—the gym during school hours and for ballgames, and the auditorium as needed.

The place looked busy with citizens coming to

cast ballots. She recognized several people from church. Barbara from the toy store. Jimmy James, the town's lovable bad boy. Tate Donovan, a member of the town's rescue squad.

Cassidy frowned as she continued to process this morning's news.

The people who'd been at Lisa's last night were the locals who supported Mac. Now a good number of them were sick and probably wouldn't be able to vote today.

The conclusions going through Cassidy's head left her uneasy in more than one way.

Could this be a case of accidental food poisoning? Absolutely. But what if it was something more? And, even if it was, how would she prove it?

"Thanks for coming out," a deep voice said in her ear.

She turned and saw Mac MacArthur standing there. The man, in his late sixties, looked nice and tidy today as he wore his best jeans and a button-up shirt. Donning a suit would have been so out of character for Mac that people would have called him out on it. No, if there was one thing Mac didn't do, it was to put on airs.

That was the very quality everyone around here liked about Mac. He was real, and he earnestly cared about this community.

"I wouldn't have missed it." Cassidy rested her hands on her duty belt. "Even if I wasn't working right now."

"The last time we had a tight race was for the town board five years ago. Two brothers were running against each other. Someone actually pulled out a gun as the family feud went over the top."

"Let's just hope that doesn't happen today."

Just through the door leading outside, Cassidy spotted another candidate, Mayor Tomlinson, greeting people as they came in to vote. The man had given this election his all over the past few days, hosting large parties, making unrealistic promises, and calling in favors from people who were on the fence. That's what Cassidy had heard, at least.

Politics could be dirty. No one would deny that.

But Mac wasn't playing a political game. No, he didn't have it in him.

What the man should be doing was enjoying retirement. But he'd seen the need to oust Tomlinson, who was only in office because of his family, long thought of as powerful here on the island.

Then Anthony Gilead had added himself to the mix.

Now everything about this election felt down-right toxic at times.

As Mac stared out over the lines of people—many

of them residents Cassidy had never seen before—his eyes lined with worry. "I heard about what happened. About Morty."

"I know. It's horrible." Cassidy couldn't stop thinking about it, couldn't stop thinking about how horrible it was that a simple get-together had led to this.

"They're investigating Lisa's now?" Mac rubbed his chin, still staring out over the crowd.

"Yes, the restaurant is closed until officials can determine what's going on."

Mac turned toward her, a tight frown pinching his lips and the election forgotten, if even just for a moment. "How's Lisa?"

"She's a mess, as you can imagine. She's afraid that word will leak and The Crazy Chefette will never be the same."

Mac looked back at the lines of people, and his gaze narrowed. "Something is going on, Cassidy."

She'd thought the same thing, but she wanted to hear Mac's thoughts on the situation. "Why do you say that?"

"Lisa has a nearly perfect rating at her restaurant with the health department. Her kitchen is pristine."

"I agree. But, as Ty said—what if this wasn't because of Lisa's actions? What if she bought some produce or meat that was tainted?"

Half of Mac's lip pulled down in a frown. "I have another idea for you."

"What's that?"

"What if someone else tainted that food just to rig the election?"

As Mac's words washed over Cassidy, a sick feeling grew in her stomach. She'd wondered the same thing . . . The idea had been teasing her, but she'd been trying to keep it at arm's length. Hearing the theory said aloud only made it more chilling.

"There's a problem with that," Cassidy said. "If it's true and the food was purposefully tainted, it will take weeks for the investigation and confirmation. This election is today. The results will be tallied tonight."

Mac's gaze darkened. "I've thought about that. Believe me, I have."

"I'm going to do everything I can to find answers, Mac."

"I know you will, Cassidy. It's good to have a person like you on my side."

But as Mac said the words, Cassidy ran through the numbers again.

There were approximately six hundred residents here on the island.

Historically speaking, only about half of those residents would actually make it to the polls today.

Voter turnout on the island had never been strong, especially since Tomlinson generally ran unopposed. More might come out today just because there was actual competition. But, for simplicity's sake, Cassidy figured three hundred people might show up.

Last night, about two hundred people had gone to Mac's party. Of those, approximately one-fourth were now sick. Maybe more. Cassidy expected others to become ill throughout the day.

That might leave around one hundred people who were staunchly Mac supporters who would come out today. One hundred would not be enough to win this election.

Meanwhile, Cassidy knew that, at one time, there had been around 150 residents at Gilead's Cove. She wasn't sure how many—if any—of them were official residents. Nor did she think that the new people who had been bused in could vote.

But, still, the numbers felt too close for comfort.

She needed to go to the town administration office. Maybe someone there could put her mind at ease.

And then she would call Ty and head to Gilead's Cove to talk to Moriah.

"I NEED a moment of your time, please." Cassidy stared at Niles Shepherd, the town manager. He'd also taken over the election proceedings after the town clerk had been murdered seven days ago.

Niles was much more difficult to work with than the previous clerk, Bob Anderson, had been. That fact made Cassidy miss Bob even more.

Niles looked up at her, not moving his head, with his trendy glasses perched at the end of his nose. The man, a snazzy dresser, had an olive complexion and curly, dark hair.

This was the first time Cassidy had been in his office, and the space surprised her. Niles had two immaculately-kept aquariums perched against the walls on either side of his desk. On the table behind him, Cassidy spotted pictures of Niles with . . . cats.

There were selfies with at least three cats. There was also a professional-looking picture of Niles holding a cat on the beach as the sun set behind them and another photo of a different cat staring out of a window, probably longing for Niles to return home.

The man was even more interesting than Cassidy had thought.

Niles's lips tightened. "What can I do for you, Chief?"

Cassidy paused in front of his desk. "I have a question about the election today. People have to be a resident of this town for thirty days before they can vote, correct?"

"Yes, that's accurate." His face twitched, as if he were annoyed.

"How exactly do you determine residency?"

He lowered his papers and sighed. "They need to have proof that they live here in town. An official piece of mail showing their address is in Lantern Beach, a photo ID, those types of things."

"Is it possible that someone could establish residency here without ever living here?"

He narrowed his eyes and tapped his pen on his desk. "What are you getting at, Chief Chambers? Why don't you stop circling the oyster and get to the pearl?"

Cassidy resisted giving him a dirty look and, instead, retained her professional demeanor. This man was so hard to work with. His snooty attitude had annoyed more than one person.

"This is what I need to know." She pressed her palms onto his desk and leaned toward him. "A lot of new people have moved into Gilead's Cove. I need to know if they're eligible to vote."

"Why didn't you just say so?" He let out a laugh with a short puff of air through his nose. "The answer is, in many cases, yes."

Cassidy blanched and stepped back. "Yes? Just like that?"

"I'm not sure what you want me to say. Yes, it's possible. All people have to do is to fill out a voter registration application and mail it to the board of elections. In one or two weeks, they'll be mailed a voter registration card. Mailing it helps to ensure they truly are residents."

"So people could, let's say, move to the old RV park where Gilead's Cove is located, supposedly live there for thirty days, and then apply to vote in this town?" Cassidy clarified.

"That's correct."

"What if they just put this town as their address before they ever move here? Is that possible?"

He shrugged. "I suppose. I mean, if someone really wanted to, they could have their bills and other mail forwarded here and open up a new checking account or credit card listing Lantern Beach as their address."

Nausea roiled in Cassidy's stomach. "I see."

"Don't look so upset. It's a good thing for the town. It's more tax income to help our infrastructure."

Cassidy repressed the retort that she wanted to shout out. Nothing about Gilead's Cove was good for this town. Nothing.

"I need more details, Niles."

"What kind of details?"

"Exactly how many people have been added to this town's numbers recently? And this isn't me being nosy. This is part of an investigation."

"Do you have a warrant, Chief Chambers?" Niles said her name as if it left a bad taste in his mouth.

"I don't have a warrant because you and I are simply having a conversation right now." More irritation pinched at her. Cassidy had never been one to kiss up to people—and she never would be, even if it made her life more difficult at times.

Niles let out a haughty *humph* and sighed. "We've probably had nearly one hundred people recently become residents of this town. I didn't realize, at the time, what was happening. They actually got driver's licenses elsewhere in North Carolina and listed Lantern Beach as their address."

Anger burned inside Cassidy. There had to be a check-and-balance system for this process. What they were doing shouldn't be legal. "Is it really that easy?"

"It is that easy. Even worse is the fact that we have on-site registration on election day," Niles said. "It's been like that for years. And for years, it didn't matter. No one registered. It wasn't a big deal."

But this election wasn't like all those other elections, and the lax regulations could ultimately lead to one man changing the face of an entire island. "You didn't think to mention this to anyone when you discovered it?"

"There are privacy laws. And it's not illegal to move to this area and register to vote. I may not like it, but it's not against the law."

"But in light of Bob Anderson's death . . ."

"I know, I know." Niles frowned again, only this time the expression actually looked sincere. As the sound of people in the hallway floated into his office, he lowered his voice. "I'm sorry. I was hoping you might ask sooner and give me a chance to share. We're town officials, and we're not supposed to have opinions on elections. But this one is making me really uncomfortable."

"If you hear anything else, I'd appreciate it if you'd let me know. Consider that my version of asking you in advance."

"Got it."

Cassidy took a step away, more disturbed as she left than she was when she'd arrived. She had a lot to sort through and little time to do so.

"Chief?" Niles called.

She paused and looked at the persnickety town manager. "Yes?"

"There is one more thing you might want to know." Niles tugged at his collar and cracked his neck. "Someone associated with Gilead's Cove just got a permit to open a restaurant . . . right next door to The Crazy Chefette."

A competing restaurant right next door to the restaurant that was the epicenter of the food poisoning . . . was that a coincidence?

Cassidy couldn't imagine that it was.

She knew one thing for certain: politics brought out the crazy in people. And there was a lot of crazy going on here in this town.

CHAPTER FIVE

TY'S MUSCLES were tight with anticipation as he walked beside Cassidy into Gilead's Cove. They'd been requested by a security guard at the front gate to leave her police vehicle at the entrance to the compound since they'd "voluntarily" been let inside.

Ty's gaze wandered to the old RV park as they followed an unnamed man toward the center of operations—a building called the Meeting Place. The structure had previously been a community center and office for the campground. Now members of the Cove met there to eat together and to listen to motivational talks from Anthony Gilead.

The thought of Anthony Gilead made Ty's stomach churn. He didn't like the man.

He glanced around at the old, moldy RVs. The gravel paths. The scattered trees.

A strange feeling always lingered in the air here. Or maybe lingered wasn't the best word. A strange feeling always *haunted* this space.

Ty tried to pinpoint the feel of the compound.

Suppressed? Maybe.

Strict? Yes.

Abnormal? Definitely.

His gut told him that the people here lived in fear. That they lived under a tyrannical leader who only made them *think* they had free will to do what they wanted.

Yet no one had come forward to press charges or to verify those things.

Maybe the residents were all too scared. But Ty hoped one day someone would break. That someone would be daring enough to speak the truth and bring the leader of this group down for good. Because Ty could spot evil a mile away, and Anthony Gilead was a constant blip on his radar.

"Look at that." Cassidy nodded to something in the distance.

The light blue bus Ty had seen earlier was parked beside the Meeting Place. No one appeared to be inside it now.

Where had Gilead put everyone onboard? Were there enough old, rundown RVs here for that many people to stay in? Ty had trouble believing that.

"Wait here," the guard muttered, leaving them just outside the doors to the Meeting Place.

As their guide opened the door to slip inside, the murmur of voices drifted out. The sound was subdued and restrained, as if the people had been instructed to remain respectful in a holy place.

Ty felt certain that the people from the bus were in there. Probably getting checked in. Processed. Initiated. Brainwashed.

Just like their friend Serena had been.

He frowned at the thought, hating how helpless he felt to rescue her. As a grown woman, she'd made her own choices. She'd decided by her own free will to come here. Though Ty was tempted to snatch Serena away and talk some sense into her, he knew he couldn't do that.

"You think we'll see Serena?" Ty whispered.

"I'd love to put my eyes on her and see for myself that she's okay."

"Me too."

Just then, the door to the Meeting Place opened, and Anthony Gilead stepped out, a wide grin on his face and pizazz in his steps.

The man wasn't out campaigning today. That could only mean one thing: he felt confident he would win.

More warning flags rose in Ty's mind.

"Cassidy, Ty . . . you two are becoming regulars around here." Gilead stepped toward them like an ostentatious host putting his best foot forward to woo an audience.

"Don't flatter yourself." Cassidy narrowed her eyes, disliking the man as much as Ty did. "I need to talk to Moriah."

Gilead's smile slipped. "Is everything okay?"

"I have some questions for her concerning an investigation we're doing."

He stared at Cassidy a moment before nodding stiffly. "Very well then. Let me go find her for you."

Cassidy turned to Ty as Gilead walked away. "That man gives me the creeps. Every time. How do people fall for this guy's act?"

Ty had spent a lot of time thinking about that very question. "He offers them something they're looking for. You experienced it yourself last time you were here. He has a way of getting inside people's heads."

His insides tightened at the thought of it. At the thought that Gilead had been able to get to his wife. Get in her head.

Gilead had cornered Cassidy inside an RV and proceeded to give her an evaluation of her fears and shortcomings. The problem was that he'd been mostly correct and had left Cassidy shaken. The farther Cassidy was away from this man, the better.

"Yes, he does have a way of getting in people's heads." Cassidy pressed her lips together and frowned.

Ty shifted his weight on the gravel, grateful that a few tall trees offered shade from the overbearing sun. In the distance, he heard scampering. Most likely, it was birds and squirrels. But what if it was the sound of residents, hurrying about in hopes of remaining unseen?

The thought caused a chill to sweep up his spine, and he stepped closer to Cassidy.

There was nothing good about this place.

A moment later, Moriah stepped from the double doors and paused, a scowl on her face.

This woman didn't look like the same Moriah Ty had first met. The old Moriah had worn an old beige tunic and khakis, just like the other followers here at the Cove.

The new Moriah wore a dress. It was long—to her ankles—and a plain blue color. But still, she stood out now against the conformity of others here at the compound.

Was this one of the privileges she received being married to Gilead? Ty would guess the answer was yes. He'd also guess that the tradeoff wasn't worth it.

"I heard you wanted to see me." Moriah's gaze narrowed at Cassidy as she stood stiffly in front of them. Her hollow gaze appeared to be laced with pride and self-preservation.

Interesting. Her accent had begun to disappear as well. She'd had a strong West Virginia dialect not long ago.

Was Gilead trying to transform her into someone else? Ty kept his thoughts to himself.

He was anxious to hear what Moriah had to say to Cassidy. Because answers were slow in coming, and they were running out of time.

———

"I NEED A WORD WITH YOU," Cassidy told Moriah. "I'm here on official police business."

Cassidy stared at the woman. Moriah was in her early twenties, but she still seemed so much like a girl. She had long blonde hair nearly to her waist. It was wavy but looked clean. Her pale skin was flawless.

And to think this woman had been married before . . . it seemed unimaginable. She just seemed so young to have experienced so much.

Cassidy still wasn't convinced that Moriah's first husband's death wasn't somehow connected with this group, even though the police in West Virginia couldn't find any link.

Moriah raised her chin, as if trying to look confident, but she somehow failed to sell it. "My husband said I could give you a few minutes of my time."

"How generous of him." Cassidy knew she should have repressed the sarcastic drip of her words, but it was too late. Gilead was obviously controlling, and Cassidy didn't want to think about what life would be like married to the man. "Is there somewhere more private we can chat?"

Moriah nodded to an area in the distance. "There are some benches over in our prayer garden. We can speak there."

Cassidy followed Moriah into a wooded area, Ty by her side. In times like these, he acted as backup in case she needed it. He'd been sworn in as an officer of the law during a case not long ago, and he still had the authority to act as law enforcement if needed.

Though he was strictly a volunteer, Cassidy found comfort in having him near. It may have something to do with the fact that he was a former Navy SEAL and more qualified to protect her than anyone else she knew. Not to mention the fact that he loved her like crazy and would do anything for her.

Moriah sat on a rough wooden bench that had probably been left from when this place was a campground. She looked up at Cassidy, no sign of warmth in her gaze. "What can I do for you?"

"I need to ask you about the incident that happened last week," Cassidy began. "I'm sure you remember calling me and asking for help. Asking me to meet you in the woods."

Moriah's façade broke for a moment, and she licked her lips.

"They forced me to do it." Her voice trembled as she said the words.

"Who did?" Cassidy listened carefully, watching Moriah's body language for any signs of deceit. The woman seemed nervous. Was the root of the reaction guilt or fear, though? Cassidy wasn't sure.

"Those men." Moriah's hand quivered as she pushed a hair behind her ear. "I was walking in the woods. I like to do that sometimes. You should know that. You saw me there before."

"I did. What happened?"

"They grabbed me. Told me if I didn't make that call to you they'd kill me."

"How did they know I knew you?" Cassidy stood on guard, occasionally scanning around them for any signs of trouble. She saw nothing and no one. Again, it was almost like there was some kind of alert system that directed people to stay inside their RVs whenever she was around.

Moriah shrugged. "I don't know. Maybe they didn't know. They just needed a woman to act helpless to lure you out here. It's the only thing I can think of."

"You're saying you'd never seen these men before?"

Moriah looked halfway offended as her eyes narrowed and her voice tightened. "No, of course not."

"So those men are not affiliated with Gilead's Cove?"

She raised her chin in an act of stubborn petulance. "We're not that kind of organization. We like peace."

Cassidy wasn't buying it. "One more question. Why were you walking in the woods on your wedding day?"

Moriah's face paled, and she remained quiet a moment. "Maybe I was having some second thoughts. That isn't unusual."

"But you did get married?" Cassidy clarified, not wanting to assume anything.

Moriah raised her chin again and smoothed the skirt of her dress. "Yes, I did. Of course. I'm honored to call Anthony Gilead my husband. He's a good man."

Moriah's story didn't make sense, but there was

nothing Cassidy could prove. Basically, it was Moriah's word against Cassidy's gut instinct. However, the men who'd been arrested had told her the same story about finding Moriah in the woods.

"Is there anything else you need to share?" Cassidy asked.

Moriah rose, her features still stiff. "No, not a thing. I'm just glad you're okay. And I'm sorry. I didn't want to drag you into their plan. I just . . . well, I felt helpless."

"They could have killed me." Cassidy needed to remind her this hadn't been a simple case of being inconvenienced. Those men had blood in their eyes. If Ty hadn't arrived when he did . . .

"But they didn't. I'm glad you were able to stop them." The quiver returned to Moriah's voice.

Cassidy knew exactly what move she needed to make next. "Very well then. I'll just need to talk to Gilead and make sure he can corroborate your story. That you disappeared before your wedding. That he's never seen these men."

Moriah's face grew paler as she clutched the fabric of her dress near her neck. "You don't have to do that, do you? He doesn't know anything."

"I'll let him be the one to tell me that." Cassidy took a step away when Moriah grabbed her arm. She paused and turned to the girl.

Moriah's eyes pleaded with her. "Please don't talk to Gilead."

Cassidy tilted her head, sensing a new fear about the woman. Cassidy had to figure out some way to get through to her. "Why not?"

"I just . . . he . . . he won't be happy."

"He won't be happy that you lured me to the woods so those men could kill me?"

Panic fluttered through Moriah's gaze. "It wasn't like that. It wasn't. But if Gilead finds out, he'll be so upset with me. If he even has the mere suspicion that it happened, whether it's true or not, he'll be mad."

Cassidy let the dust settle on Moriah's words before nodding. "I may be able to help you. But, if I do, I'm going to need your help in return."

Moriah glanced around before her wide eyes settled on Cassidy again. "What do you mean?"

"On occasion, I might need information."

"Like what?"

"All kinds of stuff. Like why Gilead wants to win this election so badly."

Moriah's shoulders sagged. "He only told me three days ago that he was running. After we were married. He doesn't talk to me about stuff like that."

Cassidy wasn't done yet. "Who are these people he's bused in?"

"I . . . I don't know that either. Honestly, I don't.

I've been gone on my honeymoon and . . ." Moriah rubbed a finger across her lips and frowned. "I did hear—not from Gilead—but I heard that they came from that town that flooded about three hours south from here."

"What town?" Cassidy said.

"A hurricane went through there in the fall and destroyed some of those small towns, leaving people without places to live or work. I heard Gilead had his people go down and tell people about the better life they could have here. They had nothing to lose by coming."

Cassidy's stomach roiled with unease. A hurricane had hit farther south of here in the fall and taken out entire towns and livelihoods. She knew people in those counties were hurting and desperate . . . but desperate enough to come here?

She hated the thought of it.

She stepped closer to Moriah and lowered her voice. "Prove that I can trust you. Tell me something I don't know about your new husband."

Moriah licked her lips, her gaze wavering. "I don't know."

"There's got to be something."

She let out a long sigh and looked off in the distance. Then realization rolled over her features. "He has scars on his back."

Ty stepped forward, something about Moriah's statement obviously catching his interest. "What do you mean?"

"I mean, his back . . . the skin there looks like raw meat." She shivered. "Only it isn't. His wounds are all healed now. But it looks like he was whipped, and his skin got ripped off and . . . it looks horrible." Moriah grimaced again.

"Did you ask him about what happened?" Cassidy asked.

"No . . . the subject didn't come up. And Gilead doesn't take questions of that sort lightly. I figured it was better if I just pretended like I didn't notice." Moriah glanced around again, guilt filling her eyes. "Now, can you please let me go? I'm already going to have to think of a way to explain this."

"What are you going to say?" Ty asked.

"That my parents are looking for me. It makes the most sense. Please, don't let Gilead know what we've talked about."

The fear in the woman's voice caused Cassidy's heart to squeeze. Moriah needed guidance from someone she could trust, not these people who were nowhere close to looking out for her best interests. "I can help you, Moriah."

Moriah shook her head, a new adamancy to the

action. "I just want you to stay away. Please. That's how you can help me."

Cassidy hated to admit it, but she was going to have to wait for Moriah to make her own choices . . . and Moriah wasn't ready to do that right now. She just hoped the woman saw the light before it was too late.

She hoped the same for Serena too.

CHAPTER SIX

TY'S MIND churned as he climbed into Cassidy's SUV. Scars? Raw meat? Just what had happened to Anthony Gilead during those missing years on his timeline?

"What are you thinking?" Cassidy asked, cranking the engine.

"I'm trying to figure out why Anthony Gilead's back might look the way it does."

"It's peculiar, isn't it?"

They started down the road. Cassidy would drop him off at Hope House so he could continue to prepare for his upcoming retreat for veterans and so Cassidy could continue working.

But right now, the conversation with Moriah was all he could think about.

Ty shook his head and stared out the window at

the balmy day outside. "I still think Gilead has a tie with my duty in the Middle East. I believe that's where he was during his unaccounted-for time period."

"I think you're probably right."

"The man just disappeared off the face of the earth for three or four years—which is really hard to do." Ty glanced at Cassidy. "Did you ever try calling his college friends? His associates? His first wife?"

Cassidy frowned, her gaze still focused on the road ahead. "No one except his mother has returned my calls. It's almost like they're afraid to talk, as was his mom."

"Gilead doesn't want people to know what happened to him during that time, does he? It wouldn't surprise me if the man had somehow threatened them." Moriah was a case in point. The woman had underlying tremors of terror in her voice and in her body language.

"No, he doesn't want people to know about his missing years," Cassidy said. "But whatever happened during that time must have been horrible."

Ty knew Anthony Gilead's real name was Gerrard Becker. He'd grown up in New Jersey. He'd shown evidence of narcissistic, maybe even psychopathic, behavior dating back as early as high school. The man had actually gone to seminary and had pastored a small church for a while before abruptly leaving. He'd been married at least twice. Neither of his ex-wives were talking.

"We're going to figure Anthony Gilead out one day," Cassidy said, her jaw twitching with stubborn determination. "I'm going to keep calling people from his past. If I had the manpower, I would go up to his hometown myself and see what I could track down. But it just can't happen right now."

Ty took her hand into his, realizing the pressure this case was putting on her. Cassidy looked so tired lately, and she tossed and turned at night. All of this was taking a toll on her.

"I know you are, Cassidy. I know you're doing all you can."

"I just wish I could figure out a way to get Moriah and Serena out of there." Her voice strained with disappointment—disappointment in herself. She put too much pressure on herself sometimes. It was hard to convince her that she'd gone above and beyond in almost every case.

"You still want to help Moriah?" Ty asked quietly. "You and I both know she's not telling the truth. She played a definite role in trying to have you killed."

Cassidy frowned, still staring straight ahead as they cruised down the road toward their cottage.

"Yeah, I know she did. She'll never admit it, but, for some reason, she wanted me gone."

"Why would she want you gone?" Cassidy had done all she could to try to help the woman.

"For some reason, Moriah must see me as a threat. And I don't necessarily like the woman. But, once you get past her outer shell, it's clear to see she's scared. Confused. Alone. But I can't do anything unless she takes the first step."

"You could arrest her," Ty said. "She had something to do with your attempted murder."

"I thought about that. But Gilead would post bail. Take her home. He'd probably kill her before she ever even got to court."

"You really think so?"

Her grip visibly tightened on the steering wheel. "I really do. I'm going to have to choose my plan very carefully here, Ty."

"I agree. I thought my situation with DH-7 was as perilous as it came, but now I don't know. Gilead's Cove is a whole 'nother kind of twisted evil."

"Agreed." Cassidy let out a sigh and glanced at him. "What's next for you today?"

"My old friend Colton Locke is coming into town for this retreat. He was on my team when we raided the compound to save that soldier who'd been abducted by Akrum Abadi. I really want to talk to him face-to-face and see if he remembers something I don't. I have a pretty good memory, Cassidy. I think I'd remember seeing Anthony Gilead, and I don't. But something has been bugging me about the man ever since I first laid eyes on him. I have to figure out what."

"Maybe Colton will offer some answers then."

Ty's jaw flexed. "I can only hope."

Not just for his safety but for everyone's.

———

CASSIDY HAD MORE work to do than she had time in her day. But before she went back to the office, she decided to swing by to check on Lisa.

Three cars with the Department of Health logo on the doors were parked in front of the restaurant. A few people stood on the sidewalk and stared.

Did they know The Crazy Chefette was at the epicenter of the food poisoning fiasco? Were they coming to gawk? Or were they just speculating about what might be happening inside?

Cassidy would find out soon enough, she supposed.

Before she climbed out of her SUV, Clemson called.

"Fourteen more people have come in," he said. "Two of them are sick. Really sick."

Cassidy frowned, realizing she was silly to hope for good news. "Sick as in their lives are on the line?"

"No, but one is . . . Ernestine." His voice caught.

Cassidy swallowed back her regret. She knew Clemson had a soft spot for the woman. Though the two weren't officially dating, they were fond of each other. And the fact that Ernestine had even come out to support Mac had been a huge step for the agoraphobic woman who served as the newspaper editor from the confines of her home.

"Oh, Clem . . . I'm so sorry. Is she okay?"

"She'll recover. It's the panic attacks she's having while at the clinic that worry me."

Cassidy squeezed her phone harder. "If there's anything I can do, let me know. Please."

"I will. I expect to hear some preliminary results from the lab soon, by the way. They assured me they'd stay on top of this. However, it will take about forty-eight hours to know for sure. The bacteria have to be cultured, and you can't speed up that process."

"I'll be waiting for your call with those preliminary results."

Cassidy stepped out of her SUV and strode toward the front door of The Crazy Chefette. The old Coast Guard building had been painted yellow, and cheerful pink shutters had been added. The Crazy Chefette sign included a cartoonish image of a blonde woman in a lab coat, holding a beaker in one hand and a spatula in the other. Under the business name were the words: mad food created by a crazy woman.

Yes, Lisa had a background that included working in a lab. Obviously, she could have cultured some type of bacteria that would cause this outbreak. But she had no motive to do so.

The heaviness of the situation pressed on Cassidy again.

She tugged on the front door and found it was unlocked. Cassidy stepped inside, unsure what she would find. Three men in hazmat suits and goggles were scouring the restaurant with evidence bags in hand.

The place looked like a crime scene—probably because it was.

One of the men hurried toward her.

"I'm sorry, the restaurant is closed—" He paused. "You're with the police department?"

"I'm Chief Chambers. I was coming to check on the situation here."

"I'm Gilbert with the Department of Health. We're trying to find the source of the contamination."

"And?" Cassidy asked, watching the men work in the dining area.

Gilbert pulled his goggles up and eased his face gear back, revealing a frown. "Unfortunately, everything has been cleaned up and cleaned up well. This place is spic-and-span."

"That's usually a good thing in the food industry business."

"It is, but it's not great for our investigations."

"So you haven't found anything?" Cassidy propped her hip against one of the tables where she and her friends often sat to eat and catch up with each other. Now everything seemed tainted. But she felt certain they would clear this up and things would return to normal soon enough.

"No, we haven't," Gilbert said. "But we're diligent, and we're taking this matter extremely seriously."

"As you should."

"Gilbert, I think I found it." Another man stepped into the dining area from the back of the restaurant, holding something in his hand.

Cassidy straightened, anxious to hear what he'd discovered—anxious for answers.

Gilbert walked toward his colleague, squinting at the flimsy white object he held in his outstretched arm.

"What is this?" Gilbert asked.

"It's a heavy-duty piping bag—like the kind used to ice a cake. It has a little bit of brown liquid in the plastic, and check this out. There's a cap on it that someone could have popped off. They could have contaminated something, and no one would have known."

"You should ask Lisa and make sure she's never seen that," Cassidy said.

Lisa was known for her creative recipes and methods of cooking. Cassidy wasn't convinced this wasn't an innocent cooking tool Lisa had used and discarded.

"What's going on?" Lisa stepped into the room, wearing sweats and an old T-shirt. She must have come from her apartment upstairs. "I heard the commotion down here. Did you find something?"

Cassidy noted that Lisa's eyes were red, like she'd been crying. She was still taking this hard. What a way to start her second week of marriage. At least Braden was understanding and kind.

"Do you recognize this?" Gilbert held up the bag.

Lisa studied it for a moment before shaking her head. "No, I can't say I do. Nor do I recognize the liquid inside. I would never put liquid into a bag like that. It's meant for icing. Why?"

The sinking feeling in Cassidy's stomach only dug deeper.

They still didn't have answers yet, but all the signs pointed to the fact that this food poisoning episode was an intentional act of malice.

CHAPTER SEVEN

CASSIDY SAT with Lisa and Braden in their apartment, far away from any listening ears downstairs. They'd gathered in the living room, Lisa and Braden beside each other on the couch and Cassidy in a chair across from them.

Lisa hadn't even offered Cassidy anything to drink or eat, which was a sure sign of her emotional distress.

And Cassidy didn't blame her. This was a worst-case scenario for Lisa.

"Did you know Austin is sick?" Lisa sniffled before grabbing a tissue and blowing her nose. "And Morty is dead. I never liked the man, but I would never wish this on him."

"Careful what you say." Braden cast an apologetic glance at Cassidy. "I mean, I know Cassidy is our friend, but she's also the police chief. No offense, Cassidy."

"No offense taken." Cassidy frowned, knowing his words were true. The last thing she'd ever want was to arrest one of her friends. But it was also her sworn duty to follow the law here in this town, despite any personal loyalties.

"Do you have any piping bags like that, Lisa?" Cassidy asked.

Lisa pulled her knees to her chest and shrugged. "Maybe I have some piping bags. I mean, on occasion I use them, even though I don't consider myself a baker. I don't even know. Why do you ask?"

"I just want to know if these guys will find the same bag down in your storage area."

Her lips parted in horror. "What will happen if they do? Will they arrest me?"

"The Department of Health can't arrest you."

"But they can file reports. They can shut me down." She squeezed Braden's hand and leaned into him, looking weak with despair.

Cassidy bent toward her friend, resting her elbows against her legs. She needed to figure this out before the drama stretched on any further. And that meant she had to ask some hard questions.

"Lisa, have you heard anything about the building that's for sale next door?" Cassidy asked.

Her shoulder rose in a half shrug. "Not really. Why? It's been vacant for years."

"Apparently, someone from Gilead's Cove has purchased it."

"Why would they do that?" Braden asked.

Cassidy hesitated before saying, "Because they want to open a restaurant."

Lisa stared back at her briefly before closing her eyes. Then she buried her face in her hands, and there was nothing anyone could do to comfort her.

AN HOUR LATER, Cassidy was still at Lisa's. Mac and Ty had also come, and they were creating a list of everyone who'd been at Mac's party. The group had moved into the dining area and sat around the table. Cassidy had pen and paper in hand as she listened to everyone spout out names.

"Is there anyone else you can think of who was at the party last night?" Cassidy asked, staring at the list in front of her.

She needed to know who may have had access to the food, who might have tainted it. They still didn't know anything for sure, but Cassidy wanted all her facts lined up, just in case.

"How many people do we have so far?" Mac asked.

"We're at 187."

"I'm sure we could be missing a few people, but I think that about covers it," Mac said.

Cassidy stared at the list. Almost all her favorite people from the island were on it. Lisa and Braden. Austin and Skye. Pastor Jack Wilson and his wife, Juliette. Wes. Mac. Clemson and Ernestine. Carter Denver. Even Jimmy James had come out.

Her department had turned out in support. Officers Billy Leggott and Dane Bradshaw. Even Melva, her antisocial, overly anxious dispatcher was there.

There was no one on the list whom Cassidy could imagine participating in something like this.

"Who had access to the food?" Cassidy asked. "I know everyone could have touched it, but who were your servers?"

"Just my usual people," Lisa said, absently rubbing her fingers across the tabletop. "Some high school girls. A couple ladies from church. No one who would do this."

"Did anyone see someone acting suspiciously around the food?" Cassidy continued.

The group at the table exchanged glances, but no one spoke up.

"There was one strange thing," Braden said. "It

might not be anything. But I saw Rebecca Jarvis bent over the food. She had an odd look on her face."

"Rebecca?" Cassidy paused. "She is the one who helped broker some of the real estate deals Gilead's Cove has made."

"Wait—you think this is connected with Gilead's Cove?" Braden sounded slightly dumbfounded as the question left his lips.

Cassidy exchanged a look with Ty and Mac. "It's all speculation. But if all of Mac's supporters come down with food poisoning, that makes it a lot easier for Gilead—or Tomlinson—to win this thing."

"I wouldn't put it past either of those two." Braden frowned.

"Let's not let that theory leave this room," Cassidy said. "Like I said, I have no proof and it's still early. We need lab tests to come back first. We all just need to be patient."

Lisa sniffled.

Cassidy reached out and put a hand on her friend's arm. "I know that's not easy—especially for you. Your business and reputation are on the line here. But trust the legal process. I'm going to do everything I can to figure out what happened here. Starting with talking to Rebecca."

Lisa nodded. "Thank you, Cassidy."

Someone knocked on the door.

"I'll get it for you," Cassidy said.

She stomped down the stairs and pulled the door open. Their friend Carter Denver stood there. He was a local musician and songwriter—and another of Lantern Beach's mysteries. No one really knew much about his past or how he supported himself, but some theorized that he'd written some hit songs and lived off royalties.

Either way, he was a likable enough guy with a killer voice and an adorably rowdy dog.

"Carter, what brings you this way?" Cassidy asked, watching his expression. He appeared pensive, which was unusual for the normally laid-back man.

He frowned. "Hey, Cassidy. I wasn't expecting to see you here. I, uh, I . . . just thought Lisa needed to know something."

"Is it about the food poisoning?"

He squirmed, his pensiveness growing by the moment. "No, actually it's not. I'm just going to lay it out there and not beat around the bush. There's a rumor going around town that Lisa stored a dead body in her freezer here at the restaurant. Is that true?"

The blood left Cassidy's face. How had word about that leaked out? The only people who knew were her, Clemson, Leggott, Lisa, and Braden.

The freezer at the morgue had died, and Clemson had asked Lisa if he could use her freezer—just for two days—to store a body connected with a case they were working. Everyone involved had been sworn to secrecy, and the restaurant had been closed at the time, so there were no health or contamination concerns.

Again, Cassidy's fears rose to the surface—fears that someone in her inner circle couldn't be trusted.

She needed to figure out what to do about that, and soon.

Until then, Cassidy offered Carter a tentative smile. "I assure you that this restaurant has superior ratings with the health department . . ."

"You didn't answer my question."

She swallowed hard. "I can't comment on cases. I'm sorry, Carter."

CHAPTER EIGHT

CASSIDY PLANNED to talk to Rebecca. But first she decided to swing past the polling location to make sure things were still running smoothly. Her foot hit the brake when the school came into sight.

A light-blue, worn-down bus was parked out front.

Dread trickled in her stomach.

Gilead had brought his army out to vote, Cassidy realized. She didn't like the way things were looking.

With trepidation, she climbed from her SUV and walked into the building. It was packed inside, and she recognized only a few people.

Mayor Tomlinson sidled up next to her as she took her place on the periphery of the gymnatorium. The man was a long-time local who acted as if he owned the island. He had a robust belly, salt-and-pepper hair, and bright blue eyes that could be charming or stormy.

"This should be illegal," he muttered.

"I agree that it feels shady."

"Can't you do anything to stop them?" Accusation stained his voice—just one more reason for Cassidy not to care for the man or desire that he be re-elected.

"I already talked to officials, and apparently everyone who's voting is here legally. There's nothing I can do." It pained her to say the words.

Tomlinson narrowed his eyes. "I know you don't want me to win and that the two of us haven't always seen eye to eye. But, Cassidy, we cannot let this man win either."

Cassidy's gaze traveled across the room, and she spotted Gilead schmoozing with voters. He grinned widely, showing his pearly white teeth. His dark hair was perfectly styled away from his face as he leaned in to people, grasping their hands with both of his and exuding warmth.

Cassidy's lips nearly curled in disgust at the sight. "If I could find a loophole to stop this, I would."

"They want to take over this whole island, you know." Tomlinson crossed his arms and followed her gaze.

"Why do you say that?" Though Cassidy had her

own definite opinions on the matter, she was interested in hearing his explanation.

Tomlinson's hands flew in the air. "It's obvious. Buying up all these properties. Moving all these new people here. Anthony Gilead wants somewhere secluded to enact whatever his plans are, and Lantern Beach must be the perfect, vulnerable location. All of this is on purpose."

"Is this speculation?" She stole a glance at Tomlinson.

His nostrils flared. His jaw tightened. His hands fisted.

"It's years of being active in politics. I can sense these things a mile away. I worry because I don't know how far Gilead will take it to get what he wants."

Cassidy had nothing to say. Because for the first time in a long time, she couldn't agree with the mayor more. But she was also reminded she couldn't rule him out as a suspect. Tomlinson had just as much reason to want to sideline Mac's followers as Gilead did.

She'd be wise to keep that in mind.

With one more glance at the crowd, Cassidy departed to visit Rebecca Jarvis. As she paused by her vehicle outside, something in the distance caught her eye.

A black Lexus had stopped behind the school building. Dane Bradshaw, one of her officers, leaned into the window and handed the driver something.

Cassidy kept watching, curious about what was going on. She'd never seen that car in town before.

As the driver shifted, Cassidy caught sight of him.

She sucked in a breath.

It was Anthony Gilead.

Just what was Dane giving the man? Whatever it was, Cassidy didn't like the conclusions that started to form in her mind.

————

CASSIDY PARKED outside real estate agent Rebecca Jarvis's humble cottage and climbed the steps to her door.

This was not the way she'd planned on her day going. There was already enough stress with the election, but with this food poisoning case, everything had tripled in intensity.

Cassidy needed answers.

Now.

Unfortunately, confirming the evidence took time. Lab results weren't always quick. And everyone didn't operate on Cassidy's schedule. The best thing she could do in the meantime was to keep searching for answers.

Rebecca answered the door, wearing an apron over her dress slacks and button-up top. The affable woman was a pretty blonde in her early thirties. She always kept herself well put together, wearing professional clothing, classic makeup, and neat shoulder-length hair.

The smell of something savory drifted toward the door and made Cassidy's stomach grumble. She reminded herself that she needed to eat today. Food often was her last priority when working a big case, but Ty and Lisa always seemed to look out for her and bring lunch or dinner by. In fact, on Tuesdays, Cassidy and her friends usually ate at Lisa's.

Sadness bit into her at the thought. That most likely wouldn't be happening today. It probably wouldn't be happening for a while.

"Chief, how can I help you?" Rebecca plastered on a smile as she pushed a stray hair behind her ear.

"I have some questions for you," Cassidy began. "Do you mind if I come in?"

"Not at all. Can I offer you something to eat?"

As the scent of the food—garlic and onions—lingered in the air, Cassidy's stomach grumbled, and she was tempted to say yes. However, she didn't have time to make herself comfortable or even to chitchat.

"No, thank you." Cassidy paused in the entry-way. "Listen, Rebecca. You were at Mac's party's last night. Is that correct?"

"That's correct. Why?" The woman tilted her head, looking honestly curious.

"Are you feeling okay today?" Cassidy asked, noticing that she appeared to have avoided the illness so many other island residents suffered with.

Rebecca let out a nervous laugh. "Oh, is that what this is about? The food poisoning? Everyone around town is talking about that. I'm feeling fine, thank you. A little nauseated, but I think that's just the power of suggestion."

Cassidy shifted. "Rebecca, I'm just going to get to the heart of the matter here. Last night, a couple people saw you bent over the buffet at Mac's party. I hate to ask you this, but please understand that I have to. Did you tamper with the food at the party?"

Rebecca's eyes widened until her silver eyeshadow vanished. "What? Me? No. Why would I do that?"

"You tell me."

"Cassidy, you've got to know me better than this. I would never."

If Cassidy had a quarter for every time someone

said that and it wasn't true . . . "Then what were you doing last night? Why the close examination of the food?"

"I just discovered I have a gluten sensitivity, so now I have to be careful what I eat. Plus, the doctor thinks I'm not responding well to anything with red meat after I got a tick bite a few weeks ago. It's very hard to know what's safe. Food allergies are the worst."

"So you were looking at the food because of your dietary restrictions?" Cassidy clarified.

"That's right." Rebecca shook her head rapidly. "Wait—are you saying this isn't a case of accidental food poisoning? Are you implying someone did this on purpose?"

Cassidy bit down, not ready to answer that question. "I can't comment on that. But about these food allergies—you didn't think to ask Lisa what was in her recipes? Wouldn't that have been easier than taking guesses?"

"She looked awfully busy. This is just going to have to be my new normal. I'm going to have to get used to doing things this way from now on. There's no one to hold my hand."

As Rebecca said the words, an alarm sounded in the distance and the smell of smoke crept from the kitchen into the entryway. "Oh, my. Excuse me a second. I think my chicken is going to be well-done."

As Rebecca scampered away, Cassidy's gaze fell on some papers left on the table by the entryway. She glanced at the kitchen and saw that Rebecca was occupied with fanning the smoke from a griddle near the sink area.

Moving a cover sheet, Cassidy read the words on the paper below.

She sucked in a breath at what she saw.

Rebecca Jarvis had owned that building beside The Crazy Chefette. *She'd* been the one who sold the place to Gilead's Cove.

It looked like Cassidy wasn't done with this conversation after all.

CHAPTER NINE

"IT'S NOT what it looks like." Rebecca fanned her face as she sank onto her couch. "You know money has been tight since my husband lost his job. I told you that the last time we spoke."

Cassidy lowered herself onto the other end of the couch, ready to get some answers. "I'm going to need more than that, Rebecca."

Rebecca wiped the slight moisture from beneath her eyes using a tissue from the box on the table beside her. "That property has been in my family for decades. It used to be an old soda fountain. I remember going there as a girl and drinking a root beer float while my granddad told me stories about finding old shipwrecks and messages in bottles."

"Sounds like wonderful memories. Then why sell?"

"Jim and I are strapped for cash. The real estate market isn't exactly booming this time of year. I had no other choice."

"You had no choice but to sell to Gilead's Cove?" Cassidy clarified.

Rebecca shrugged and her lips pulled downward in an all-encompassing frown. "It's sat there empty for years, and they were the first ones to make an offer. Not everyone wants to take on a project like that, not when there are other buildings available that require less renovation."

"What kind of offer did Gilead's Cove make you, exactly?" Cassidy wanted to believe the best about this woman, but contrary evidence was stacking up. First, Rebecca's suspicious behavior at the party. Now, another affiliation with the area's infamous cult.

Rebecca frowned. "It's personal."

"I need to be upfront with you, Rebecca, and let you know that you're now at the top of my suspect list. You don't have to tell me, but there's a good chance I'm going to bring you in for questioning if I don't get some answers soon."

Rebecca held her stomach, her face looking green. She jumped to her feet and took off toward the hallway. The next thing Cassidy heard was the sound of her throwing up. A moment later, Rebecca reappeared, a blue hand towel pressed to her mouth.

"Are you okay, Rebecca? Do you need to go to the clinic?"

She lowered herself back onto her couch and shook her head. "No, I'm fine. I get nauseated when I'm stressed. I've been like this since I was a teenager."

"If you're sure."

"I am." Rebecca's pleading gaze met Cassidy's. "Please don't take me to the police station. No one will ever want to work with me again. Being a real estate agent means maintaining an upright reputation."

"Then please start talking. All I'm here for is the truth."

Rebecca fanned her face again, either because of unshed tears or because of the smoke still lingering in the air. "A few members of Gilead's Cove came to me with an offer that was twenty thousand below what I actually wanted."

"And you said yes?"

"I was going to say no, but . . ." She fanned her face, as if trying to ward away tears.

"But what?" Cassidy knew there was more to this story, and she was anxious to find out what.

"But they said if I sold them the land at that price

that my husband could have a job cooking there. We love cooking together. It would give Jim a new sense of purpose. He's been so mopey lately, and I just can't stand to see him like that."

"Rebecca, I'm still not liking how any of this sounds. If you have stake in a new, competing restaurant, then you seem like the most likely person to want to sabotage the competition."

"But I would never do that! I'm not that kind of person. Ask anyone who knows me."

Nice people commit crimes every day. Cassidy kept that thought quiet for now. "Can anyone verify these allergies you have?"

"Ask Doc Clemson. He did the tests. I give you my permission. You've got to believe me."

"I will be checking in with him. But I'm going to have to ask you not to leave town. We're also going to need to search your place."

"Search it all you want. You won't find anything. I'm innocent, and I have nothing to hide."

"Then, if you don't mind, I'm going to call one of my officers and get busy."

———

THREE HOURS LATER, Cassidy hadn't found

anything to indicate Rebecca was guilty of contaminating the food at The Crazy Chefette.

Cassidy glanced at her watch. It was almost six. The polls would be closing in one hour, and five more people had been admitted to the clinic this afternoon. Clemson had called in extra help from the neighboring towns so he could care for everyone. Some patients had been sent home after being tested and given fluids. But the clinic was still packed.

Cassidy had sent Officer Billy Leggott to question everyone there and see if anyone else had seen anything at the party yesterday.

Apparently, one person had seen someone sneeze on the food.

Another person noticed their neighbor didn't eat and wondered if that was an indication of guilt.

Another person swore that it was shrimp salad that was bad because she kept burping it up.

Cassidy paused from searching the kitchen cabinets at Rebecca's place and took a deep breath. Rebecca had gone for a walk on the beach while her place was being searched, and Cassidy had promised to be discreet.

She rubbed her temples, trying to ease the tension there and clear her thoughts. She wondered how Lisa was holding up. Wondered if the inspectors from the Department of Health had discovered anything new.

Wondered how the votes were looking. So much was up in the air.

Cassidy glanced at her phone and saw she had no new messages. Her mind raced back to the threatening text messages she'd received. She'd gotten three messages last week and two this week.

Each message made it clear that someone knew Cassidy's real identity and, when the time was right, they would expose her. She leaned against the kitchen counter and closed her eyes.

A ticking clock on the wall in front of her reminded Cassidy that she was on borrowed time. She didn't know who was sending these texts or what they wanted. If they really wanted to expose her, then why didn't they? Why draw it out and keep toying with her?

There was only one reason she could fathom: to prolong her agony.

"Chief."

Cassidy turned toward Dane. She'd called him to help search, partially so she could keep an eye on the man. She hadn't forgotten about his meeting with Gilead but had decided not to ask him about it. Not yet, at least.

"Yes?" Cassidy turned toward him.

He pulled his latex gloves off. "I didn't find

anything. I've searched the areas where you directed."

"Thank you, Dane. I didn't find anything either." She wiped her brow using the sleeve of her shirt. Rebecca's house was surprisingly warm.

Dane studied Cassidy's face. "What now? Are you arresting Rebecca?"

"We don't have enough evidence. It's all circumstantial."

"She doesn't seem like the type to do something like this."

"That doesn't mean she didn't. We all have a dark side. If we're pushed hard enough, we're capable of doing things that seem unthinkable." As Cassidy said the words, she remembered the first time she'd taken a life. It had been by accident.

Raul Sanders, the leader of the deadly gang DH-7.

Cassidy had been defending herself when a baseball she threw hit the man in the chest and stopped his heart.

She'd been dubbed by some as Commotio Cordis —a condition where a hard jolt stops the heart. Some in the underground had drawn cartoons praising her, and she'd become somewhat of an urban legend.

She didn't feel like a legend. No, even though Raul had been evil, it was hard to get past the fact that her actions had taken another's life. She had to live with herself each day knowing that.

No one here knew those details about her old life, her old identity. No one except Mac and Ty.

If locals knew, how would it change the way people viewed her? Certainly, some would think Cassidy was a hero. Others would think she was unfit to be police chief. Sometimes, she didn't know how she felt about it herself.

"Chief?"

She looked up and realized Dane had said something. She'd drifted off, carried away by her thoughts, by the ghosts of her past. "I'm sorry. What was that?"

"I asked what you wanted me to do now."

She glanced around. They'd done everything they could do here at Rebecca's place. "I think we're done. I'll tell Rebecca she can come back in. We'll file our report and wait for the lab results to come back and see if there are fingerprints on the piping bag. There's really nothing else we can do."

As if on cue, her phone rang. It was Clemson again.

"I was just going to call you," Cassidy said.

"Rebecca said you would, and I can confirm that she does indeed have some food allergies."

"Good to know. I have a feeling that's not why

you called, though." Cassidy shoved the phone between her shoulder and head as she slipped off her gloves.

"Good instincts. The preliminary lab results are back. This looks like a case of salmonella, Cassidy. I wanted you to be the first to know."

CHAPTER TEN

TY WATCHED as Cassidy leaned closer to the computer before taking a bite of the chicken salad sandwich he'd brought her. It was dinnertime, and he knew Cassidy would forfeit eating if he didn't bring her food. He'd made a sandwich and packed up some fruit and a bottle of water. It wasn't the heartiest dinner, but it would work.

"I can't believe this, Ty," Cassidy muttered as she wiped some crumbs from her lips with a napkin.

Something else she couldn't believe? She'd told Ty about Dane, and he was still reeling from that update. Could Dane really have been the leak this whole time?

If so, he'd put Cassidy's life in danger. That made Ty want to have a one-on-one talk with the man.

But he would reserve his judgment. The man hadn't been proven guilty yet.

"What is it?" Ty asked.

Whatever Cassidy had discovered, she looked outraged with her hunched shoulders and puckered lips.

"You can actually buy salmonella samples online. Anyone can."

"For real?" Ty stood and leaned over her, his eyes scanning the website. Sure enough, she was correct.

Cassidy leaned back and shook her head. "So, basically, anyone can buy these samples. They can culture them in their home or in a lab. And then they can use their final product against people."

"That is pretty crazy to think about. And it definitely doesn't help narrow down your suspects, does it?"

Cassidy frowned. "Not at all. Anyone could have done this. I know I've said that several times, but I just can't believe it."

"Or this could have been accidental. It could have been in produce or meat. We can't rule that out yet."

"I have a feeling that piping bag they found in the trash at The Crazy Chefette is going to prove someone did this on purpose. My guess is they had no idea someone would die from the outbreak. They just thought people would get sick and it would deter them from voting."

"But if someone did this on purpose, it's now more than food poisoning, isn't it? Couldn't this be involuntary manslaughter, at least?"

Cassidy nodded and leaned back in her squeaky desk chair. "I'd say so."

Ty sat back down across from her and crossed his arms. "First, we have to hope that we get more results and soon. The health department has probably taken samples of most of the food. They should be able to pinpoint the source."

"And, hopefully, we'll find some fingerprints on that piping bag—if it really is the source of this outbreak." Cassidy pursed her lips again, not touching the rest of her food. "I keep imagining it playing out, Ty."

"What do you see?"

She closed her eyes. "I can picture someone slipping that bag beneath their sleeve—if the bag wasn't too full, it would fit perfectly. All this person would have to do is take the top off, lean over the food, and let the salmonella drain out into the food. They probably mixed their sample with some liquid to make it easier to combine. They could quickly stir it in, and no one would ever know. It could happen that fast."

Ty's stomach hurt just thinking about it. "It's actually pretty scary to think about."

"I agree. I'm really glad you didn't get sick." She ran her hand across the side of his face before lowering it back into her lap and offering a sad smile. "I feel so bad for everyone who did."

"I think we all do. Especially for Morty."

"Isn't that the truth?" Cassidy stood.

"What now?" As he said the words, he heard the front door open.

Cassidy stepped toward the doorway, and recognition lit her face. "It's Gilbert from the health department. Maybe he has an update as well."

"WE'RE ABOUT to head out of town. I think we've got everything we need," Gilbert said as he stood in Cassidy's office with the door closed. Ty had stepped outside to give them privacy.

Cassidy raised her eyebrows. "Already?"

Gilbert helped himself to some water from the cooler set up against the wall. He took a long sip before nodding and answering. "The test results aren't back yet, but we questioned the people who became ill and were able to pinpoint one common food source. It appears that the salad dressing was contaminated."

"That can't be a coincidence." Cassidy crossed her arms as she thought everything through. "I know it's too early to say for sure that this was purposeful, but, when you put all the facts together, I think we can all agree it's the most likely scenario."

He crumpled his cup and tossed it into the trash-can. "I'm inclined to agree with you. Someone did this on purpose with the intention of causing a lot of people to get sick. I've worked this job for a long time, and I've never seen anything like this."

"I haven't either. But at least this clears Lisa. Correct?"

Gilbert tensed and tilted his head. "Not necessar-ily. I suppose that's for you to determine. We just investigate the source of the illness."

Cassidy knew with certainty her friend wasn't behind this—because she knew Lisa. "Then let me talk through a few things with you. Why would someone purposefully contaminate food at their own restaurant? What sense would it make?"

"We don't know. That's what we're trying to find out. People have done crazier things."

Cassidy couldn't argue with that.

"We got some fingerprints from the piping bag,"

Gilbert continued. "You'll need to send them to the lab."

"I will. But if Lisa handled the piping bag then her prints could be on it."

"That's true."

Cassidy didn't like where this was going. All the evidence seemed to point at her friend—at least from Gilbert's perspective.

"This needs to be solved and soon," Cassidy said. "Especially with the election going on today. This event will definitely affect the outcome. There's no way it won't."

Gilbert frowned and got another cup of water, taking another long sip before tossing the new cup. "There's one other thing I think you should know, Chief."

"What's that?"

His frown deepened. "Given the number of people who've gotten sick . . . and the fact that this was done on purpose . . . this is really out of our hands. This is considered bioterrorism. I've put in a call to the FBI, and they're coming here first thing in the morning."

Cassidy blinked in surprise. The FBI?

Yes, this day could most definitely get worse.

CHAPTER ELEVEN

THE WHOLE GANG met at Cassidy and Ty's place to await the election results. Lisa had originally volunteered to bring snacks, but no one could blame her when she changed her mind. Instead, Cassidy had picked up some chips, dips, and cookies from the general store before heading home.

Lisa's food would have been much better, and not having it here served as a grim reminder of what had happened.

"How's Austin?" Lisa asked Skye, Austin's girlfriend.

They all stood around the breakfast bar, munching on snacks and chatting. More than anything, Cassidy wanted it to feel like it always did when the group was together—laid back and fun. But she could feel the tension in the air.

Skye shook her head, her dangly earrings hitting her neck. She hadn't quite been the same since her niece Serena had joined Gilead's Cove. It seemed as if everyone here had their own sorrows, their own issues.

"Austin is still weak," Skye said. "He's at his place resting. I'm going to check on him when I leave here. He insisted I should come and support Mac, though. He's really upset that someone would do this."

"The whole island should be upset." Wes rubbed his hand over his head, his short hair almost making him appear bald. "Bioterrorism? Here on Lantern Beach? That's not supposed to happen."

"Whoever did this is going to be in a whole heap of trouble," Mac said, his normal glibness gone with the winter weather on the island. "This is about more than rigging a small-town election. This is about harming a community."

"You're still going to win this, Mac." Braden squeezed his shoulder. "We believe in you."

Mac didn't look convinced. He frowned. This was obviously bothering him.

Cassidy clapped her hands, trying to add some lightness back into the group. "Why don't we all grab a plate of food and move out onto the deck. We should be getting a phone call from Niles any time now with the results, and it feels great outside."

But no one seemed particularly enthusiastic as they filled their plates. Lisa didn't bother to eat at all.

"You do have to eat something." Cassidy sat down beside her. She knew she had little room to talk, but worrying about others came more easily than worrying about herself.

"I just don't have much of an appetite."

"This is going to pass."

"Everyone knows about the dead body, Cassidy."

Cassidy licked her lips, knowing she had to tell the truth. "I heard. I've been talking to everyone who knew about it, but no one is taking responsibility for the leak. But I'll figure it out."

"Even if the food poisoning passes, I'm not sure that will." She buried her face in her hands.

"Tourists aren't going to know about it. They're the bulk of your business in the summer. And then by the fall, everyone local will forget."

She looked up, tight lines on her face. "Someone already mentioned it in an online review."

Cassidy frowned. "What? Already?"

Lisa nodded. "There are people who get pleasure by bringing other people down and making them look bad. I wish I could say that stopped after high school, but it doesn't. Some people never grow up."

"Maybe you can get whatever site it is to take it down."

"Maybe." But Lisa sounded unconvinced.

"I never did get to hear about your honeymoon." Again, Cassidy tried to change the subject to something light, a distraction from everyone's problems.

The first real smile seemed to cross Lisa's face. "It was wonderful, Cassidy. I just feel so lucky to have found Braden. I can't imagine my future without him."

She caught his gaze from across the room, and they shared a grin. Cassidy was so happy her two friends had found each other.

"And Cancun? Was it wonderful? I've heard it's beautiful."

"It was the best. The beach was perfect, and we got to just relax."

Cassidy wasn't sure why, but her thoughts drifted to Moriah and Gilead. Could Moriah say the same thing about her honeymoon? Cassidy couldn't see that being the case, though she could be wrong.

As much as she wanted to stop thinking about this case, she couldn't. There was so much on the line for so many people.

And if Gilead won this election, it would be like the first domino in a long line had been tapped, sending everything else around falling and spiraling as the bigger picture finally came into view.

———

TY PULLED Wes back into the kitchen to help with drinks. He kept one eye on the rest of the room through the open windows and door.

"Did you hear any scuttlebutt about what happened today?" Ty asked.

Wes had a good pulse on the area. Though he wasn't exactly a social butterfly, people on the island liked him. He did plumbing work at many of the homes here, and people knew they could depend on him.

"Everyone has been talking about the food poisoning. For the first time in my life, I don't feel guilty about not eating salad."

Ty's gaze went to Cassidy as she patted Lisa's back. Her compassion for others while in the midst of her own turmoil was just one of the many reasons he loved her.

"What else did you hear?" he asked Wes.

"That Rebecca Jarvis might be behind this."

Ty frowned. "Word of that leaked too?"

"Someone drove past and saw the police cars parked outside her place. I guess they put it together." Wes studied his face. "You think Gilead's Cove is behind this, don't you?"

Ty wouldn't deny it to his friend. "They make the most sense. I mean, I wouldn't put it past Anthony Gilead to do something like this."

"I wouldn't either. He just looks like a dirty politician. I get the creeps whenever I see him in town. But do you really think Gilead feels like he'll get away with this?"

Ty pictured the man. As usual, his muscles tightened at the thought of the man's smug grin. "It's hard to say. I think Anthony Gilead has been really good at covering his tracks in the past. I have no doubt he was connected with some of these other crimes that have happened since he moved to the island. He's just really good at keeping his hands clean."

"Makes me scared for the future of this town."

"You're not the only one." Ty knew so much could change if the wrong person was in power. If Gilead won, his whole cult might take over this island and drive everyone else away. The thought was disturbing on more than one level. And it was just one more reason why Mac had to win.

Mac's phone rang, and everyone in the room quieted.

Ty fully expected Mac's face to light up in a grin

as he learned of his victory. Or, at least, Ty had fully expected that just twenty-four hours ago.

But Mac's face showed nothing now. He only offered a series of grunts and affirmations. When he ended the call, he glanced around the room at everyone present.

All eyes were on Mac as they waited to hear confirmation that he had won.

"Well?" Wes asked, breaking the silence first.

"I didn't win," Mac said, his voice as emotionless as his expression.

A scattering of gasps and mutterings of grief went around the room.

Ty stepped forward. "Who did?"

Mac frowned. "Anthony Gilead is your new mayor."

CHAPTER TWELVE

MORIAH DIDN'T DARE MOVE. She remained perfectly still as she lay in bed, unwilling to let her husband know she was stirring. It was still dark outside. If she had to guess, the time was about 5:30. She had a tendency to wake up at the same time every morning, and that's what time her internal alarm clock told her it was.

Gilead's back was toward her—his bare back. She stared at the mangled lines there. Moriah knew she shouldn't be fascinated by the sight of his scars, but she'd never seen anything like them.

One day, she would be brave enough to ask him about the grotesque marks that made his skin look like ground beef.

As if he could feel her eyes on him, Gilead turned over, the sheets rustling beneath him. He smiled when he saw Moriah but made no move to scoot closer. He didn't like cuddling. That's what he'd told her.

"Good morning, my love," he said.

"Good morning."

"How'd you sleep?"

It had been a terrible night of sleep. Maybe it was the mattress. Moriah knew that wasn't the case, even though she tried to convince herself.

It had been her thoughts that kept her from resting—her realization that she'd made a terrible mistake when she married Gilead.

Just like she'd made a terrible mistake when she'd married her first husband, Vince. After she'd left West Virginia, he'd apparently been murdered.

Speaking of Vince . . . just yesterday, Moriah had wandered into Gilead's office and seen the strangest thing. She wasn't supposed to be in there. She definitely wasn't supposed to be snooping. But she'd needed a flashlight.

She'd come across a paper that almost looked like a life insurance check. It had been made out to Moriah, but she'd never gotten any notice about it. She'd had her mail forwarded here. Had Gilead intercepted the check and kept it for himself?

No, he wouldn't do that.

Yet part of Moriah wondered if he would. After

all, the check had been for nearly one hundred thousand dollars. That was a lot of money. People did crazy things for that amount of cash.

"I slept fine," Moriah finally said, trying to keep the conversation simple.

"Good, I'm glad to hear that. You need some rest if you're to get your to-do list done today."

"My to-do list?" Though she'd done chores yesterday evening, she'd hoped that schedule wasn't permanent.

"Yes, of course. Everyone has a job here."

"But I thought—"

Gilead raised a brow. "What? That since you were married to me, you'd be exempt?"

Moriah said nothing.

"No, my dear. If I have the job of leading this place, then you do also."

"But I cleaned yesterday." She hated the whine that crept into her voice. But she had to wonder if this was Gilead's way of punishing her for talking to Cassidy yesterday.

"And today I'd like for you to scrub this room down with cleanser. On your hands and knees. It's the only way to ensure it really gets clean."

Tears nearly sprang to Moriah's eyes at the thought. "Gilead, my knees are sore from scrubbing the bathroom yesterday."

That had been her task in the afternoon. Gilead had given her a toothbrush and locked her in the room. She couldn't leave until Gilead approved of the job she'd done. And he was picky. There had been some gunky dirt in a corner, and when Gilead had found it while inspecting the space, Moriah had been forced to start all over.

Moriah had hardly been able to breathe because of the fumes from the cleanser, and she hadn't been able to eat until she was done. Gilead had said it would be a good lesson for her in thoroughness. Told her that cleanliness was next to godliness. Had reminded her that wives were to obey their husbands.

It was nearly midnight before her work passed Gilead's inspection. By that time, the kitchen was closed.

Moriah felt lightheaded from hypoglycemia. She desperately needed food, but Gilead didn't seem to care. His main concern was that she learned her lessons.

After he'd fallen asleep, Moriah had snuck downstairs into the community kitchen and found some leftover bread. She'd eaten four pieces and finally felt better.

The truth echoed in her mind. If Moriah went into shock, no one here would get help for her.

Instead, she would probably die a slow, painful death.

"Are you arguing with me, Moriah?" Gilead's voice took on a sharp tone.

Her neck stiffened on the pillow. "No, I'm not arguing. I just—"

"It sounds an awful lot like arguing." His eyes narrowed. "I need for you to set a good example for the others here at the Cove. If my wife doesn't obey me, why should anyone else?"

"But there are other people here who can do this —" Her voice took on a desperate tone.

"But I asked you. My wife. I can read some more verses to you about obedience if you'd like."

She closed her eyes for a moment. She'd heard enough of those yesterday. "No, that won't be necessary. It's just that I'm sore—"

"Moriah," his voice hardened. "I've already given you a chance to stop arguing with me, yet you continue. Get out of bed."

Her heart thumped in her chest at the bitter sound of his voice. "But—"

"I said get out of bed. Now."

His tone left no room for argument. Moriah scrambled out of bed and stood, waiting for his next instruction. Her beige nightgown brushed her knees, and her cold legs missed the warmth of the covers. It was still springtime, and an early morning chill filled the air.

"Do you see that spot on the floor in front of the bed? The red paint has been worn off, leaving a mark."

She glanced down and saw the wear spot. "Yes."

"Stand there."

She didn't ask questions, even though she wanted to. Instead, she did as she was told.

Gilead sat up, propping the pillows behind his head. "Put your feet together."

She did.

"Hands to your sides," he continued.

She obeyed.

"I need to hear some affirmation here."

"Yes, sir," Moriah whispered. What kind of woman had to say *yes, sir* to her husband? Tears wanted to pop to her eyes, but she couldn't let them. Gilead wouldn't approve, and she could only imagine how he might react. He was already on edge.

"Now, I want you to stand there, perfectly still, until I say you can move."

Her knees wobbled at the thought, and her stomach grumbled again. "Could I get something to eat first—"

"You just added more time to your punishment. You're to be silent."

Moriah clamped her mouth shut and stood there.

As she did, Gilead turned on the lamp beside the bed and picked up the book from his nightstand. It was a Bible. He opened the Good Book and began reading. Occasionally, he lifted his eyes to check on her, to make sure she was being obedient.

The first hour was challenging. Moriah didn't think it would be. How hard was it to stand? It shouldn't be that difficult. But she felt so, so tired. She just wanted to sit down. To rest. To get a bite to eat.

But she didn't dare speak. She needed to end this subtle torture as soon as she could.

She considered crying out for help, but it would be of no use. For starters, everyone thought Gilead walked on water. They would side with him.

And secondly, all he'd asked Moriah to do was to stand in one place. That didn't sound nearly as torturous as it felt.

But she was just weary. She needed to go to the bathroom.

You don't have to do this, she reminded herself. She could refuse. Stand up to him.

But she feared what Gilead would do to her if she did. He wasn't the type to let her walk away.

Moriah watched Gilead, her handsome husband. The man she'd dreamed about marrying. He looked so intent as he read, appearing calm and cool and like this was nothing out of the usual.

He was a con artist, she realized. Someone who could promise people the world, but Moriah would never have imagined marriage to him would be like this.

She was trapped. She had no money. No car. Even if she could get out of the compound, she'd have nowhere to go.

Cassidy Chambers, she remembered. The chief had offered to help her.

But Moriah had set the woman up to die. Could the police chief really be trusted? What if the woman just wanted vengeance? Moriah wouldn't blame her, if that was the case.

Moriah had been so jealous. She'd thought Gilead was interested in Cassidy Chambers, and Moriah had wanted him all to herself.

She'd been so wrong. So, so wrong.

Two hours later, after Moriah's knees had nearly buckled and the sun had long since risen, Gilead closed his Bible and stood. "Are you ready to do what I asked now?"

Moriah didn't dare move anything but her lips. "Yes, sir."

He smiled. "Very well then. I'm glad you can see things my way."

He stepped closer, pausing in front of her. The next thing she knew, his lips consumed hers. Instead of melting into his embrace, all she wanted to do was run.

CHAPTER THIRTEEN

CASSIDY ARRIVED at the police station bright and early that morning to meet the two FBI agents who were coming to take over the investigation. It was bad enough that the North Carolina State Bureau of Investigations had taken over her last two investigations, but the FBI took it to an all new level.

This case was no joke.

Bioterrorism?

The person who'd done this would be in a lot of trouble.

Cassidy purposely slipped into her office a few minutes ahead of schedule and closed the door so she could gather her thoughts. But only one resounding thought stayed in her mind.

Anthony Gilead had been elected mayor.

She leaned back in her chair, still trying to let that sink in.

How was this even possible? She needed to speak with someone higher up in the local government than the town manager, Niles Shepherd. She needed to speak to someone with the county and figure out how this food poisoning case would affect the election. There had to be some way to stop any proceedings.

Because Cassidy felt sick at the idea that Anthony Gilead might become her boss. That he might be in charge of this town. That he might get away with whatever he was planning.

She lifted a prayer before opening her eyes and digging into her day.

To start, Cassidy called Clemson, who informed her they were down to only ten patients at the clinic. Everyone else had been sent home. The ones left were the most vulnerable—the elderly, one child, one person in remission from cancer. They needed to be monitored and kept on fluids.

As she hung up, Cassidy briefly considered calling Lisa but decided to let her friend sleep instead. It was only 8:00, and Lisa probably needed her rest after the day she'd had yesterday.

Last night, since she'd been unable to sleep, Cassidy had looked online and had read some of the mean reviews people had left of The Crazy Chefette.

Bad for your health.

The owner is crazy, that's for sure.

She keeps dead bodies in her freezer. Who knows what she's really putting in the food?

Though Cassidy felt confident the restaurant would bounce back, she also understood the stress this must be putting on Lisa as the owner and chef.

It only increased her urgency to find answers.

Who could be behind this? Cassidy pulled out a pen and paper to jot down some notes and try to sort out her thoughts.

Rebecca Jarvis remained a suspect in Cassidy's mind. Even though they'd found no evidence that the woman had tainted the food, Rebecca had the best motive, and she was associated, by default at least, with Gilead's Cove through her real estate deals.

Even though Gilead had won the election, Cassidy also needed to consider the idea that Tomlinson could somehow be involved. He also had a motive, and the man wasn't the most scrupulous to walk the earth. His plan could have backfired, leading him to still lose.

Cassidy searched through her file and found the handwritten list of people who'd been at Mac's party. She reviewed the names again but still had no other ideas as far as suspects. She needed more information first. Maybe the FBI could provide her with that.

By the end of the day, they should have affirmation on the salmonella and possibly even the strain. Right now, they only had preliminary results from the lab.

Cassidy rubbed her eyes. It was never a good sign when her eyes were tired before 9:00 a.m.

Someone knocked on her door. Cassidy looked up and saw Melva standing there. The woman, in her late fifties, had a grandmotherly look about her with her short, poofy hair and old-fashioned clothes.

"Good morning, Chief."

"Hi, Melva." Cassidy squinted as she noticed the roller still at the back of the woman's hair. She started to tell her, but Melva's pensive expression made her pause. "Is everything okay?"

"I've been nervous about eating anything ever since this epidemic broke out on the island." Melva wrung her hands together, one of her signature quirks. "I saw how sick some of those people were. I don't want that."

"Investigators believe they've found the source of the food poisoning. I don't think you should worry." Besides, Cassidy believed the motive had been to rig the election. Now that the results were in, there was no reason for someone to strike again.

Melva looked so nervous that a pang of sorrow rushed through Cassidy. It must be horrible living with so much anxiety all the time.

"What's happening to this town, Chief?" Melva's lips twisted in distress.

Cassidy was certain Melva's thoughts echoed many people's on Lantern Beach. "I wish I knew. Hopefully, we'll have some answers soon."

"You keep saying that, but there haven't been any answers." Melva's gaze was actually steady and halfway accusatory as she met Cassidy's. Eye contact usually wasn't the woman's strong suit.

Cassidy frowned at Melva's words. She wanted to rebuke them, but she couldn't. They were true. Ever since the madness in town had started, Cassidy had been reassuring everyone there would be an end.

That hadn't happened yet. In fact, the waters were only growing murkier.

"I'm doing my best, Melva."

The woman grimaced, and her shoulders drooped. "I didn't mean to imply you weren't. It's just that my daughter and granddaughter are supposed to come to town in two weeks. With every-thing going on . . ."

"I didn't even know you had a daughter, Melva.

You never really talk about yourself much." Cassidy hadn't seen any pictures or anything. In fact, she knew very little about the woman outside of what happened here at the office.

Cassidy knew Melva's husband had died about six years ago, and he'd made good money working for a company called Huntington Rawlings in Raleigh before moving to Lantern Beach and taking a job at the pier. He'd traded the daily grind for the simpler life. That's what Melva had told Cassidy when Cassidy had first taken the job here.

Melva shrugged. "I guess I never think people are interested. When you've been a widow for as long as I have, you get used to being ignored."

Sadness clutched Cassidy's heart. "I'm so sorry, Melva. I had no idea you felt that way."

She should have been more diligent and reached out to the woman more. But Melva had seemed reclusive and nervous around Cassidy. Around everyone, really. Cassidy had just assumed she wanted to be left alone.

"It's okay. I'm glad I get to work here. It gives me something to keep my mind occupied."

Cassidy silently vowed to do a better job. She didn't want anyone she knew to feel that kind of loneliness. Not if she could help it.

"There's one other thing, Chief." Melva frowned, wrinkles forming around her mouth.

"What is it?"

"I wasn't sure if I should mention this or not. But on three different occasions, I've seen a car outside my house. I don't want to sound paranoid, but I think someone is watching me."

The air left Cassidy's lungs. "You should have told me sooner, Melva. Did you see anyone inside the vehicle?"

She shook her head. "No, it was a black sedan with tinted windows. It could be nothing."

But it could be something. "I'll have Leggott drive past your house and keep an eye on the situation. If you see this car again, call me right away."

"Do you think I'm in danger, Chief?" Melva's voice broke.

"I don't know," Cassidy told her. But she did worry that maybe, for some reason, the woman might just be a target.

Before they could talk any more, the doors opened in the lobby, and Cassidy spotted two men in suits step inside.

The FBI.

She really hoped they had an update on this investigation.

TY HEARD a vehicle rumbling into his driveway and hurried down the front steps. Just as he reached the concrete, an old Ford F150 pulled to a stop beneath his house, and his friend Colton Locke stepped out.

Colton Locke . . . thirty-two years old, with a swoop of dark blond hair coming down over his forehead, tan skin, and a fit military build and demeanor. He was one of Ty's closest friends, and they'd bonded in a way only the battlefield could provide.

A grin lit Ty's face. It had been a long time since he'd seen his friend, and Ty was glad Colton had been able to come early for the retreat.

"Colton, my man," Ty said, giving him a bro hug. "How are you?"

"I can't complain." Colton stepped back and grabbed a duffle bag from the truck bed. "It's good to see you. It looks like marriage is agreeing with you."

"I highly recommend it—if it's to the right person, of course."

"Yeah, man. One day, I'll meet the right woman. But it hasn't happened yet."

"I heard you had a whole lot of women lining up to date you. You were just too picky to say yes."

"Hey, if there's no indication we could have a future together—that we can have fun together—

then there's no need to go any further. You know what I mean?"

"Yes, I do. Come on." The truth was, Colton's heart had been broken after he'd returned from his time overseas with his injuries. When his girlfriend had seen what the road to recovery would be like, she'd decided not to stick around. Those emotional injuries had probably been more damaging to his friend than the IED blast he'd endured.

Ty waved his hand. "Let's get you set up in one of the cabanas."

Colton glanced around, his gaze sweeping to the cabanas behind the house, over the driveway, and then to the sand dunes in front of the cottage. "This place looks incredible. You've done good work here, Ty. I've only heard good things about your program."

"If the good Lord is willing, I'll keep it going." Ty had a scare earlier in the year. He'd run out of funding after some flooding, but the needed money had come through at the last minute.

As Colton flexed his arm to throw his bag over his shoulder, Ty spotted the burn marks on his bicep.

It was a near miracle Colton hadn't lost a limb or an eye in the explosion. But he had experienced weeks of painful surgeries to graft the skin on his arm, shoulder, and part of his chest back together.

Afterward, he'd gone through months of excruciating therapy to regain use of his body.

Still, Colton hadn't let any of that slow him down.

Once Colton's baggage was in a cabana at the back of the property, he and Ty went into the main house and grabbed a drink. They sat on the screened-in porch and kicked back for a minute, catching up on life.

When there was a break in the conversation, Ty leaned forward, a question pressing on him. "Colton, there's something I need to ask you."

"Sure, man. What is it?"

"It's not going to be a pleasant memory. I wouldn't bring it up if it wasn't important."

Colton's eyes narrowed. "Is this about that terrorist compound we raided?"

"It sure is."

"I think about that rescue every day."

"So do I. And I'm afraid my past has come back to haunt me." Ty stood. "Let's grab our rods and tackle. This conversation may take a while. We might as well catch dinner in the process."

CHAPTER FOURTEEN

CASSIDY LEANED BACK in her chair, feeling at ease as she spoke to Special Agents Fielding and Easton. Both were likeable and professional—a stark change from her encounters with Agent Abbott from the NCSBI.

The two reminded her a bit of Bert and Ernie. Fielding was tall and thin, while Easton was shorter and stouter. Fielding was a talker, while Easton was quieter.

They were seated in a small conference room at the station. Cassidy sat at the head of the table, and the two agents sat on either side of her. She'd had Melva bring in a pitcher of water as well as some homemade trail mix Lisa had given Cassidy a couple of days earlier. It contained Lisa's signature crazy touch—ordinary trail mix with nuts and chocolates and a surprise addition of bacon and Old Bay.

Cassidy gave the two agents the rundown on what she knew, and then waited, hoping they'd share something.

After a moment of hesitation, Fielding spoke up. "We are treating this as a case of bioterrorism here on Lantern Beach. So many people became ill by this act, and the fact that it appears to be purposeful . . . it's not like anything I've seen in my ten years of being an agent. Usually food poisoning is accidental."

"I agree. I never expected something like this to happen here." Nor had she expected to ever hear the words "bioterrorism" and "Lantern Beach" in the same sentence. It seemed surreal.

Easton leaned forward. "As you know, we're still waiting on definitive findings, but we want to proceed. We feel confident the final results are going to match the preliminary conclusions. That means someone in this town wants to harm a lot of people for some reason. Is there anyone you can think of who matches that description?"

Cassidy didn't hesitate to tell them about Gilead's Cove.

"Do you think this is another Waco?" Fielding asked. "A David Koresh situation?"

Cassidy shrugged. "It's hard to say. The group

makes me uneasy, but so far, I haven't been able to pinpoint them doing anything illegal. I have suspicions they're careful to keep clean hands with whatever they're doing."

"We'd be happy to assist in any way we can," Fielding said. "And definitely talk to the county about the election. As you're well aware, election fraud is a serious crime."

Cassidy was sure Anthony Gilead would claim innocence. There would be no trail leading back to him—only to someone associated with him. That was the way the man operated.

"It sounds like this place, being a small town, is a hub of criminal enterprises," Fielding leaned back and grabbed another handful of trail mix. "And, by the way, this trail mix is surprisingly addictive."

She didn't tell them Lisa had made it. Instead, Cassidy nodded, figuring the less they knew, the better. "I was surprised when I came here also."

"Where'd you come here from?" Fielding asked, wiping his hands on a napkin and pushing the trail mix away.

A surge of anxiety rose in Cassidy at his question. Though she had a cover story, the last thing she needed was for people to dig into her past and start asking questions. She'd thought the job here in Lantern Beach would be low-key enough that things like this wouldn't be an issue. But life had other plans, apparently.

"I'm from Texas. I didn't actually have much experience when they hired me, just a desire for justice and a good nose for finding answers." Cassidy smiled, trying to look relaxed.

Fielding's eyes lit. "I'm from Texas. What part?"

"A little town named Impact."

"The smallest town in Texas." Fielding's voice lifted with excitement.

She blinked, trying not to show any panic. "That's correct. I can't believe you've been there. Hardly anyone has heard of it."

"I actually dated a girl from that area. You ever met Valerie Clark? I'm sure you have in a small town like that. Doesn't everyone know each other in those kinds of places?"

Cassidy opened her mouth, about to respond—except she didn't know what to say. Deny it, and it would look like she hadn't lived there. Affirm his words, and she could get caught in a lie.

Thankfully, Fielding's cell rang and delayed her response.

He grunted into the phone and glanced at his partner. As he ended the call, he turned to Cassidy. "We got some prints back on that piping bag."

Her breath caught. "Did you? They matched someone in the system?"

"As a matter of fact, they did. Someone named Dane Bradshaw."

Cassidy nearly choked on the air. "Dane? Are you sure?"

Fielding nodded. "Positive."

———

TY CAST his fishing line over the pier and then leaned back in his red camping chair, waiting for the first bite. Colton did the same beside him.

The day was perfect—not too hot, not too cold. The sun shone brightly above them, and even the birds seemed to be rejoicing that summer was getting closer. They flew in circles above the pier, squawking and diving and putting on a show for anyone watching.

"So, how has life been treating you?" Ty started, trying to ease into the tough conversation ahead.

Colton shrugged. "I can't complain. I miss the military, though."

"It's a hard transition sometimes, isn't it?" Ty had experienced it himself and seen it frequently in others.

"It really is. You get used to the adrenaline rushes,

you know? As a SEAL, life was always changing and you never knew what adventure to expect next. You were out there saving the world and nearly dying in the process. Then you're thrust back into civilian life where your biggest concern seems to be finding the right house and figuring out what to cook for dinner. It's enough to give a person an identity crisis."

"You sound bored."

Colton shrugged again and slipped on some sunglasses. "I don't know. Maybe I am. I mean, my therapy after the injury took up a lot of my time. When it was over . . . well, it's been hard to find a new sense of purpose. I know some of the guys have families they're trying to acclimate to."

Colton's words sounded harsh, but they were true. It was hard for a lot of people in the military to return to everyday life—especially life with a family. For the months they were gone, their loved ones operated without them. Then they came home from deployment or missions, and sometimes their children who were so young when they left now barely remembered their military parents. Their spouses were used to making choices on their own. It was definitely an adjustment for all involved.

"Braden has been talking to me about branching out from Hope House." Ty felt a tug on his line and reeled it in. Seaweed dangled from the end. "He thinks I should go the paramilitary route, and once guys have recovered and been approved, offer them jobs here in the States."

"Doing what?"

Ty pulled the plants from his hook and cast his line again. "Bodyguard work. PI work. You know the drill. There are plenty of other organizations like it."

"So what would make yours different?"

Ty leaned back and slowly nodded in thought. "That's a great question. I think it would need to be a total life overhaul if people committed to it. You know, it wouldn't be a matter of me sending guys out there just to do jobs. There would need to be accountability. Monitoring. Following up to make sure these people's lives were on track. You and I both know how hard it could be."

"I have to say, if there's anyone who can do it, I think it would be you, Chambers. You've got a knack, and you're a natural leader." He pushed his sunglasses up higher.

"I'd need help if I did it, though. I can't run Hope House and start another branch too."

Colton glanced at him. "You hinting at something?"

Ty raised a shoulder. "Maybe. I know I can't go forward unless I have the right team around me—a team of people I can trust. People like you."

Colton said nothing for a minute, only stared out over the water, before finally saying, "I like the idea of it. I'll think about it and pray on it."

"You do that." Ty stared off over the water at the white-capped waves gracefully curling toward the sandy beach in the distance. He wished his thoughts felt as carefree as the ocean did. But there was too much on his mind.

"So, about that last mission we went on . . ." Ty started, his voice hoarse with bad memories.

"I don't think any of us will ever forget it."

"Yeah, I think you're right. Seeing a human in the state we found that guy in . . . it changes your life." They'd found a man—a soldier—who'd been captured and nearly beaten to death. On the man's back, there had been a maze of scars from the whippings he'd received. Ty had never seen someone in such a state before. It was something he'd never forget.

"It does. Why are you bringing it up now? Did something happen?"

"Colton, is there anything in particular you remember about that rescue? Anything out of the ordinary that bugs you about it?"

"That's kind of vague. A lot about it bugs me."

Ty filled him in on Anthony Gilead.

Colton pulled his sunglasses down and stared Ty

in the eye. "So you think this Anthony Gilead guy is somehow tied in with that mission and he came here because of you?"

"I know it sounds crazy," Ty said. He'd thought the same thing. "I really do. But there's some connection, and I can't figure it out."

"That's not like you. You're a sharp guy, and you've got a great memory for details."

"That's why I feel like I'm missing something."

Colton's rod bent, and he stood to reel in his catch. Whatever was on the other end of that line, it was big. Colton was a strong man, but it took several minutes of struggling before the hook popped out of the water, a red drum flopping on the end.

Several people stopped to gawk as Colton pulled the fish from the hook and put it in a cooler. After some banter with the other fishermen, Colton put new bait on his line and cast it again.

The lighthearted moment quickly faded from memory, and somberness washed over them both again.

"There's one thing about that mission that really haunts me," Colton finally said. "I remember as we were leaving with the guy we rescued, I looked behind me. There was this one man standing there wearing full terrorist garb. I drew my gun, ready to defend myself. I thought he was going to shoot and try to stop us. Then I realized he wasn't armed."

"What happened?" His heart pounded in his ears. This was the first time Ty had heard about this.

"I waited to see what he would do. I couldn't see his mouth—it was covered—but it was like he was trying to tell me something."

"Why do you say that?" Ty's curiosity reared.

"I don't know. It was the look in his eyes. It was like he was pleading for help."

"What did you do?"

"As much as I would have liked to arrest all those terrorists, it wasn't our mission. I brushed it off and kept going. We had to get our guy to the helicopter. I knew if we wasted too much time, these guys could sabotage our only means of escape. I couldn't let that happen."

It was typical of their missions. They had to focus. There was no room for error. Little room to go off plan.

"Where was I when this happened?" Ty asked.

"You were beside me, holding our guy. I doubt you looked back."

"You never brought it up before?"

"Why would I? The man was a terrorist. We don't feel sorry for them. I figured he was probably trying to lure me back so he could ambush us."

"Maybe."

"But there was one thing I thought was weird about him," Colton said, his jaw tightening.

"What's that?"

"This guy had blue eyes. You don't see a lot of people in the Middle East like that."

Blue eyes? Anthony Gilead had blue eyes.

What was going on here? Was this the clue Ty had been searching for?

And, if it was, why had Anthony Gilead been at that terrorist compound? Why had he been dressed in terrorist garb? Or was that just a coincidence?

He didn't know. But he needed to find out.

CHAPTER FIFTEEN

TODAY WAS Dane's day off, and Cassidy knew he'd planned a trip to Hatteras Island so he could kiteboard with a friend. The timing worked out well, giving Cassidy, Fielding, and Easton an unobstructed opportunity to search his house for evidence.

With warrant in hand, Cassidy accompanied Fielding and Easton as they combed through Dane's living quarters.

Her mind raced.

Dane had been at Mac's party. Plus, he was privy to all the information that came into the police department. He could easily be the spy she suspected was in their midst.

She didn't want to believe it. Then again, she didn't want to believe *anyone* she trusted could betray her.

But Dane was from Ohio. He hadn't lived far from the West Virginia/Kentucky border, where Gilead had started his crusade to recruit people for his cause.

And the man had picked, out of all the places in the country, to come to Lantern Beach and apply for a job. Maybe it wasn't a coincidence. Maybe Dane had purposefully chosen this place, not because he'd always dreamed about island life, but because he was doing Gilead's bidding.

Cassidy's stomach churned at the thought.

She glanced around. She'd never been at Dane's place before. He lived in a small cottage—smaller than most of the residences around here. There were two bedrooms and a great room. It almost looked like it had originally been set up as a fishing cabin—something that wasn't intended for big family vacations but only as a place to sleep and get rest between excursions.

He hadn't done much to decorate or add many personal touches. There were a few signs that his dog, Ranger, lived here with him—a food and water bowl, a bag of dog food, a dog bed. Several Cincinnati Reds items had been placed on a shelf.

Everything appeared normal.

Please don't let it be Dane, Cassidy prayed silently. He was her first hire. He'd been by her side as she'd gone through some sticky situations. She wanted to believe the best in him, to believe the best in everyone around her.

But she couldn't be naïve either. She had to remind herself of that over and over.

She stood against the wall, observing as Fielding and Easton scoured the residence looking for clues. Cassidy had agreed that if they allowed her to be present, she would stay out of their way. It was generous of them to include her. This was a federal case now, and they weren't obligated to share anything.

Dane had no idea they were here. He had no idea what was unfolding at his house while he was away enjoying some time on the water.

Cassidy rubbed her arms, fighting uneasiness at this whole situation. Why would Dane's prints be found on that piping bag? It didn't make sense.

He hadn't gone through the dumpster behind Lisa's restaurant—Cassidy hadn't told him to, at least. But maybe there was another explanation for all this. Cassidy had to give him the benefit of the doubt, at least.

"Guys, come see this." Easton stuck his head in through the front door.

Cassidy joined Fielding as they walked outside. He'd been digging through Dane's trash. As they got closer, he reached his gloved-hand into the black garbage bin and pulled up something.

It was a petri dish. Several of them, for that matter. The kind that could be used to culture something like salmonella before infecting the food at a restaurant.

Cassidy squeezed her eyes shut. It looked like Dane really had been the one behind this.

Relief that they'd finally found answers clashed with disappointment inside her. How could Dane have done this?

———

CASSIDY LEFT while Fielding and Easton continued searching Dane's place. Though part of her wanted to stay, she knew she had other work to do.

Besides, Cassidy wasn't ready to believe Dane was behind this. She would keep looking for answers until she felt satisfied justice had been served.

She stopped by the town administration office and paused when she stepped inside.

Little stuffed cats had been placed in various places along the entry. They hadn't been here before.

Stuffed cats? What in the world was going on here?

She wandered past them and knocked at Niles's door. He scowled when he looked up at her.

"Another spot of bright sunshine for my day," he muttered.

"I take it things aren't going well so far." Cassidy stepped inside.

"My coworkers thought it would be funny to 'cat' the whole office."

Cassidy hid her amusement. "Why would they do that?"

He shrugged. "Because it's my birthday."

"Happy birthday."

"I don't celebrate birthdays." His eyes narrowed even more. "And there's nothing wrong with a man who likes cats."

"Not at all. I'm sure they were just trying to be nice."

"They could have been nice by respecting my wishes and leaving me alone." The words came out as a growl. "Now, why are you here? I suppose I can guess. The election, right?"

"That's correct. I'm uncomfortable with the results considering everything that went on here in town yesterday."

"You and everyone else."

Cassidy shifted her weight. "So you've heard other complaints?"

He lifted his eyebrow. "I've been on the phone all morning."

"And what's your professional opinion on all this?"

He let out a slow breath through his nostrils. "I'm looking into it. It is suspicious that so many people had food poisoning. But until we have something official from the police or health department, there's not much I can do. I did take this to the county board of commissioners. The good news is that we have two weeks until Anthony Gilead will be sworn in. We have some time before he takes office."

A shadow filled the doorway. Cassidy turned and saw Mayor Tomlinson standing there. He also scowled when he spotted Cassidy. Coming to this office was going to start giving her self-esteem problems.

"Chief Chambers," he said. "I was wondering if you'd come by today."

"Sorry to hear about the election."

"Me too. Of course I wanted to win. But if I lost, I didn't want it to be to Anthony Gilead, a total outsider."

"Our problem isn't just that he's an outsider. It's that he's a cult leader who likes to influence people to do what he wants."

Tomlinson rubbed his chin. "Do you think he's behind the food poisoning?"

She remembered the evidence at Dane's house. "We're still working the case."

"Well, keep working it. Because we're going to run out of time if we're not careful."

CHAPTER SIXTEEN
____

BACK IN HER office thirty minutes later, Cassidy paused as she heard the front door to the station open. Cassidy heard Melva offer a tentative greeting, her voice cracking more than usual.

It was the deep voice that floated into Cassidy's office that sent a chill down her spine. She knew exactly who was here. Her muscles stiffened at the realization.

She paced to her door and crossed her arms. "Anthony Gilead. What brings you by?"

He offered a bright smile as he stood by Melva's desk wearing his designer suit and sporting magazine-ready hair. "As I'm sure you heard, I'm going to be the new mayor of this town. I thought it would be a nice gesture to swing by and meet some of the town's leadership."

A sickly feeling roiled in Cassidy's gut. "You didn't need to waste your time. We've already met."

"But not in this official capacity." He stepped into her office and closed the door, a new boldness to his gaze. "Our relationship is going to change, Cassidy."

Heat climbed up her neck. She didn't like the way Gilead had pushed his way into her office, nor did she like the tone of his voice. "It's Chief Chambers. And we have no relationship to change. You're merely going to be mayor."

His eyes gleamed with amusement, and he appeared unaffected by her words. "I do like that fire in you. It's probably why you make such a good police chief. I can see why you were hired, even though you didn't have any previous experience in law enforcement. It was a risky move, don't you think?"

Cassidy's muscles tensed even more. Was he hinting at something? That he knew about her past?

She kept her face void of expression as she replied, "It turns out I just have a knack for this kind of work."

"I guess you do." He stepped even closer.

Cassidy was tempted to back up, to get away from him. But she stood her ground, not wanting to give the man the upper hand.

"I look forward to working closely with you, Cassidy," Gilead murmured.

Something about the way he said the words, about the way he looked at her . . . it made Cassidy feel exposed. Like she was a victim without ever being attacked. It made her like the man even less.

"At least that makes one of us," Cassidy said.

Again, her words didn't affect him. No, Gilead had come here to gloat, and he was doing just that. "I think together we can make some changes to this town."

"Most people like it just the way it is."

"But I feel confident it can be improved. That we can come together as a community and help make people's futures even brighter. Most people think of a vacation as a place to get away physically. What they don't realize is what they're craving is a restart in life. I can help with that."

His words turned Cassidy's stomach. "I don't think you were elected because people wanted a self-help guru to come in and make demands of them."

"I would never make demands. I consider them gentle encouragements."

"That's not your job. Your job is to govern this town."

He leaned closer. "I'm going to be in charge soon.

And nothing is going to stop me. Not even you, Cassidy Chambers."

———

AN HOUR LATER, Cassidy still felt uneasy. More than uneasy. She was disturbed. Anxious.

She just had a really bad feeling about this whole situation.

And what if Gilead was right? What if there was nothing Cassidy could do to stop him? He would soon be the man in charge.

Sure, there was a check-and-balance system in place, but had it ever really been put to the test in Lantern Beach? She doubted it. That laid-back attitude might cost this town its very existence in the end.

As someone knocked at her door, she stood. Agent Fielding waited outside her office.

"We've had an agent monitoring the ferry, waiting for Officer Bradshaw to return. He just pulled up to his place, and we're headed out to arrest him."

The unease in her stomach continued to grow. Why was Dane back from kiteboarding so early? She hadn't expected him to return until tonight. "Thanks for letting me know."

"Do you want to come?"

Did she want to come? Absolutely not.

But Cassidy knew she needed to. Dane was her officer, one of her people.

"Yes, but I'll drive myself. Just let me grab my keys."

A few minutes later, she was in her SUV, headed back toward Dane's place. Part of her felt sorry for Dane—and doubtful that these accusations were true. It just seemed too easy for the seasoned officer to be implicated. He would have been more careful.

But another part of her, when considering that Dane might have done this, was filled with anger. If he was guilty, then he deserved to be locked up for a long time. He'd gone against his oath of office and endangered more than one person.

In fact, someone had died because of this incident, this crime. It was no joke. No, this had been a carefully planned and executed contamination by someone who'd intended to make people sick.

Cassidy parked her SUV behind Fielding and Easton's FBI sedan. She joined them as they walked up the steps. Inside, Cassidy heard Ranger barking, announcing their arrival.

Dane opened the door before they even knocked. He still wore his wetsuit, and Ranger stood guard beside him.

Dane's hands went to his hips, and he squinted as he looked at them.

"Chief, what's going on?" His gaze latched onto hers as a deep burrow formed between his eyes. "My equipment broke, so I'm back early from—"

Before he could even finish his sentence, Fielding began reading Dane his rights and cuffed his hands behind him.

Shock washed over Dane's features, but he didn't resist. He only stared at Cassidy, his voice rising. "What? You can't think I did this? Cassidy, tell them."

She swallowed hard. "Dane, the evidence . . . I'm sorry."

"The evidence? There's no evidence. If there is, it's because I've been set up. I didn't do this. Tell them, Cassidy."

She felt helpless as she stood there, watching the agents lead Dane away. He would be kept at her jail tonight.

"Take care of Ranger for me," he called.

Cassidy nodded and took the dog's collar. "Come on, boy. You're going to stay at my place tonight, okay? Kujo will love having you there."

But as she climbed into her vehicle, she wondered if Dane's words were true. What if he had been set up? Because Dane would be smarter than to leave evidence in his trashcan. To leave his prints on the bag.

Before Cassidy could think about it much longer, her phone rang. It was Lisa, and she was sobbing.

"Cassidy, Morty's son came in, and he was so upset. He said I killed his father." She let out another sob. "What am I going to do?"

"Stay right there, Lisa. I'm coming over. I just need to make one quick stop first." Cassidy patted the top of Ranger's head, his smooth fur calming her if just for a moment.

CHAPTER SEVENTEEN

AFTER CASSIDY DROPPED off Ranger with Ty, she headed over to The Crazy Chefette. Lisa had her head buried in her arms as she sat at the diner-esque bar stretching across the back of the restaurant. Braden stood beside her, rubbing her back, speaking in soothing tones and looking overall concerned.

"Thanks for coming," Braden murmured, glancing at Cassidy. "Lisa is really upset, as you can tell."

Cassidy nodded as she slid into the seat beside Lisa. As she did, the scent of lemon and cinnamon teased her senses. Lisa's unique personality and foods and scents were just some of the many reasons Cassidy loved her.

Cassidy softened her voice as she leaned toward her friend. "Hey, girl. What happened?"

Lisa raised her head, but her face was a swamp of moisture and red blotches. Braden handed her a napkin, and she wiped her eyes and nose.

"It was so horrible, Cassidy." Her voice broke, and she wiped her eyes again.

"I can tell." Cassidy squeezed her friend's arm. "Why don't you start from the beginning?"

Lisa shifted and drew in a deep breath. "I was cleaning the kitchen—because cleaning makes me feel better. I heard someone knock on the door. I figured maybe it was a tourist who hadn't heard what happened, coming to ask what our hours were or something. But when I got there, I saw it was Frankie Simpson."

"That's Morty's son?" Cassidy had met the man once. Truthfully, she'd *arrested* the man once. He'd been driving under the influence.

He was in his mid-thirties and had a mean streak. He'd been a surfer as a teen, and all the hours he'd spent in the sun, as well as drinking and smoking, had sped up his aging process. He might be in his mid-thirties, but he looked and sounded closer to fifty with his leathery skin and gravelly voice.

"Yes, it's Morty's no-good son." Lisa sucked in a deep breath as if gathering the energy to continue. "He came in here yelling at me. It was so horrible."

"What did he say?"

When Lisa said nothing, Braden spoke up for her. "Frankie said she killed his father. He was ugly and in her face. I heard the commotion while I was upstairs and came down to . . ." Braden cleared his throat. ". . . escort him out."

Braden was a big guy, and Cassidy wondered just how he'd *escorted* Frankie. She wasn't going to ask, though. She didn't want to know. Although she felt bad that Frankie had lost his father, Frankie certainly deserved whatever rough treatment he got.

"I'm sorry, Lisa," Cassidy said, worried about her friend and the stress she was under right now. "I can imagine how hard that was for you. Don't listen to Frankie. He's just grieving, and he wants someone to blame."

Lisa sniffled again. "It's not just Frankie. It's the whole town. I feel like every time someone sees me, all they're thinking about is what I've done—even though I didn't do it. Everyone thinks I'm guilty and that my restaurant is tainted."

"That's going to change soon," Cassidy said. "We've made an arrest."

Lisa pulled her head up, and her wide eyes met Cassidy's. "What? Really?"

Cassidy nodded, though her spirit still felt heavy about it all. "We did."

"Who? Who did this?" Lisa sounded breathless as her bloodshot eyes bored into Cassidy's.

Cassidy licked her lips, trying not to show her uneasiness. "Dane Bradshaw."

Lisa gasped, and her hand flew over her mouth. "Your officer?"

"That's all I can say right now. The FBI stepped in. This is bigger than this town or this state even. A matter like this is of national concern."

"I know I should feel relieved but . . ." Lisa turned away again, staring off vacantly at the kitchen area.

"I feel the same way," Cassidy said. "I want to feel some kind of victory here, but I don't."

"Why would he do something like that?" Braden's eyes narrowed as he addressed Cassidy.

"The only thing I can think of is that he's secretly working for Gilead, and this was Dane's way of helping him win the election. That's all speculation at this point, of course."

"Dane? Working for Gilead?" Braden repeated. "I mean, I don't know the guy that well, but the few times we've spoken, he seemed like an all-right guy."

"I agree," Cassidy said. "We're just starting to dig into this more. I don't have all the answers yet. And please don't let this information leave this room. I don't want to rake his reputation over the coals if . . ."

"If he's innocent," Braden finished.

Cassidy nodded. "That's right. But I'm sure it will all come out soon, and people will forget it happened here at your restaurant, Lisa."

"And the restaurant opening next door?" Lisa asked, still appearing deflated despite the update.

Oh, yes, the old soda fountain. Cassidy couldn't forget about that. "I wish there was some kind of criminal enterprise behind it that might close the place down. But I don't think that's the case."

"Besides, there's room in the town for lots of restaurants," Braden said, resting his hand on Lisa's back. "There already are several. One more won't hurt anything."

Lisa shrugged, looking unconvinced. "I know. I really do. I just don't like this."

Cassidy didn't like it either and wished there was a magic button she could press to reset things or make life easier. "Listen, I'll tell Frankie to stay away from you. In the meantime, maybe lie low. Don't answer the door—let Braden do it for you. Okay?"

Lisa nodded. "Okay. Thanks, Cass."

"It's no problem." Cassidy stood.

Braden walked her to the door and stepped outside behind her. She sensed he had something to say and paused in front of her SUV.

Braden frowned, looking ever protective of his

petite wife. "Listen, I know you said Dane has been arrested, but I have the impression you don't buy his guilt either. Am I right?"

"There are a lot of reasons I'm skeptical." Cassidy studied him, anxious to hear what he had to say. "Why? What's going on?"

He lowered his voice. "I haven't told Lisa this yet because she has too much on her mind. But a couple weeks ago, I was down at the pier fishing. Frankie was there. In fact, he was talking to someone near the bathroom and didn't hear me come up. I left with the distinct impression that Frankie has a drug problem and that he owes someone a lot of money."

She let that sink in for a moment. "What are you saying?"

Braden shrugged. "Frankie was Morty's only living relative, right?"

"As far as I know, that's correct."

"I'm just saying, have you ever wondered if Frankie did this, knowing about his dad's health problems and knowing this would most likely be the outcome? Knowing that maybe he'd get some life insurance money?"

Cassidy let out a doubtful grunt. "If that was the case, why give everyone food poisoning?"

"Maybe he didn't mean to."

Cassidy chewed on that thought for a moment.

Even if Frankie did have a motive, she wasn't sure the rest of the story fit. "I can't picture Frankie buying salmonella and culturing it, you know?"

Braden looked across the parking lot and scowled. "I agree. It does seem like a stretch."

"And how about the evidence we found at Dane's place?" Cassidy asked. "Why would Frankie implicate Dane, of all people?"

"I might have an idea for that also." Braden shifted, as if uncomfortable. "Frankie was being really mean to his girlfriend a couple weeks ago while he was eating at The Crazy Chefette. Nothing that would get him arrested or anything. But he was talking down to her. I was about to step in, but Dane beat me to it. They went head-to-head, and I was afraid the two were going to fight."

"I'm surprised I didn't hear about that one." It seemed like something someone might mention to her.

"Nothing happened. Frankie and his girlfriend, Becky, left. It might have given Frankie a reason to hate Dane, though."

"You're right. It's worth looking into." And Cassidy knew she wouldn't get a good night's rest until she had answers.

———

SINCE CASSIDY'S department was now down to only one officer, she took Leggott with her to question Frankie. She'd hoped to talk to Dane, but the FBI agents were still with him. No doubt their questioning would take a while.

The normally quiet Leggott was full of questions as they drove.

"You really think Dane did this?" Leggott pulled his inhaler from his pocket and took a puff. It seemed that either allergies or stress caused his asthma to flare up.

Cassidy would guess that it was stress causing the reaction right now.

She shrugged, not wanting to give her opinion. Not yet, at least. "We just have to go through the process. Innocent until proven guilty, right?"

"But you found petri dishes in his trashcan? Is that true?"

Cassidy's grip tightened on the steering wheel. "That's correct."

Leggott swung his head back and forth. "I just can't see Dane doing this."

"I have trouble believing it also. But that doesn't mean he's innocent." Her words had a grim undertone.

"This is all messed up. This whole town feels

messed up. Maybe I should have left when I had the chance."

Cassidy did a doubletake as she glanced at the man. This situation was taking a toll on him as well, wasn't it? "You always have the chance, Leggott. Not that I want to see you go, but I don't want to keep you anywhere you don't want to be, either."

"I can't leave you now." Leggott let out a heavy sigh—not one that was lined with defeat but with burdens. "When you came on as police chief, I told you I'd stay for a while."

"And I appreciate that."

"I've learned so much under you, Chief. But this town is starting to creep me out. And now Anthony Gilead is going to be mayor? I can only imagine what he has in store."

"You and me both." Cassidy pulled to a stop in front of Frankie's house. Actually, it was Morty's house. Frankie had lived with his dad.

The place was rundown. Unlike most of the houses on the island, this one wasn't built on pilings. Instead, there was a low, exposed crawlspace beneath the structure. Probably a fourth of the cedar shingles appeared to have fallen off the siding, and the yard was unkempt with tall sprigs of grass and what appeared to be trash from an overturned can.

Cassidy climbed out and stepped onto a rickety

porch, which was also missing several boards. Stray cats circled the area.

With Leggott at her side, Cassidy knocked at the door. A moment later, Frankie answered, wearing a stained white tank top and looking like a proverbial redneck.

"Can I help you?" He eyed Cassidy then Leggott and put down a beer bottle on a table just inside the door.

"Hi, Frankie," Cassidy started. "We just need a few minutes of your time, please."

He still looked suspicious of them as his eyes wavered back and forth from Cassidy to Leggott. "About what?"

"Your father's death," Cassidy continued. "We're sorry for your loss."

A little of the worry left his gaze. "I don't have anything else to say about it. I just want to be alone and grieve."

Unfortunately, that couldn't happen. "I promise we won't take much of your time. But this is important."

There were many different approaches Cassidy could take, but she'd decided to go low-key right now. If the man was innocent and grieving, there was no need to add more stress to his situation.

He mumbled something beneath his breath,

crossed his arms, and finally said, "We can talk here."

"Frankie, we heard you went into The Crazy Chefette today and accused Lisa of killing your father," Cassidy said.

"The poisoning happened in her restaurant. Makes sense that it was her fault. The buck has to stop somewhere, and it was her food that did my father in." Accusation sharpened his tone.

"I assure you that we have all our resources looking into who did this," Cassidy said. "But we can't have you going around threatening people."

His lip twitched up in a sneer. "I want justice for my father."

Cassidy glanced behind Frankie, something inside the open door catching her eye. "Looks like you got a new computer there."

His eyes widened, and he scooted in front of Cassidy to block her line of sight. "What's it to you?"

"I heard money was tight. It's just surprising. I heard that brand in particular is pretty expensive."

"It's none of your business."

"I was just making small talk."

His finger jutted out toward Cassidy. "I know how you think and operate. This isn't small talk. You're implying that I killed my father. Why would I do that? So I could get the life insurance money?"

Cassidy licked her lips, proceeding carefully. "I

did hear that you were in some debt. Some drug-related debt."

Frankie stepped closer. "Look, I did some stupid things in the past. I admit it. But I wouldn't kill my father. And, even if I was that kind of person, I wouldn't kill anyone by planting something in their food. I'm a lot simpler than that."

Cassidy couldn't argue. She didn't think that Frankie would have the know-how to purchase a salmonella sample, culture it, and then figure out a subtle way to contaminate food at a party.

"Besides, my dad didn't have life insurance," Frankie said. "You can look into it yourself and you'll see."

Cassidy couldn't rule Frankie out completely, but he wasn't at the top of her suspect list. Not right now, at least. But she would double-check about that life insurance policy.

"Thank you for your time." Now Cassidy wanted to go talk to Dane. Maybe he had some answers. But mostly she hoped he had a really good, solid reason that would explain his innocence.

CHAPTER EIGHTEEN

THE AGENTS WERE STILL INTERROGATING Dane when Cassidy arrived back at the office. She had some time to kill until she could talk to him.

Spontaneously, she stopped by Melva's desk. "Listen, I'm having a couple people over for dinner tonight. Why don't you come?"

Ty had already called and said he was cooking the fish he and Colton had caught. Mac was stopping by, but Cassidy wondered if she should invite Leggott and Melva to build some unity here in the department.

Besides, Melva had said someone had been watching her. That got Cassidy's wheels turning. What if someone planned on snatching Melva to get information from her? Out of everyone in the department, she was the most vulnerable.

Cassidy didn't know how likely it was, but she needed to keep a close eye on the woman. Melva was one of her people, and Cassidy would look out for those under her care.

"You want me to come over and eat with you?" Melva repeated, blinking as if she'd misunderstood.

"Yes, at eight. Does that work for you?"

She glanced at her watch. "Yes, I can do that. Thank you for asking. I don't get too many invitations like this."

"We'd love to have you. I'm glad you can come."

Cassidy excused herself and sat at her desk for a few minutes to sort out her thoughts.

This was what she knew so far.

Someone had ordered salmonella samples, cultured them, put them into a piping bag, and somehow slipped the salmonella into the salad dressing at Mac's party. More than fifty people had reported being sick as a result—though others were also ill but hadn't come into the clinic—and one person had died.

Rebecca Jarvis remained a suspect. The woman didn't seem like a cold-blooded killer. But Cassidy could picture her being naïve enough to do something without thinking through the full consequences. Maybe Rebecca had never imagined this many people would become sick. That Morty would die. Maybe she'd been convinced it was an innocent prank. She had the opportunity to taint the food at the party, and her motive could have been financial. But that would mean she was working with Gilead's Cove.

Frankie Simpson was also a suspect, but Cassidy couldn't envision him being bright enough to put something like this together. He was more of an impulsive type of guy. But he had more of a motive here—to get his father's money. Cassidy had checked into Morty's life insurance—there wasn't any. But that didn't mean that Morty had no net worth. Frankie also had the opportunity—he was at the party. But did he truly have the means?

Then there was Dane. The petri dishes had been found at his place. He was at the party. He was smart enough to put things together, but he was also smarter than to leave the evidence in his trashcans. And he'd been seen talking to Gilead.

Cassidy's gut told her that all of this went back to Gilead's Cove. There had to be some connection with Anthony Gilead. He'd gotten someone to do this to throw the election in his favor.

Could he have influenced Dane or Rebecca to taint the food?

It was a possibility.

Would they ever admit to it if he had?

Probably not.

That man knew how to cover his tracks.

And he would be her boss soon.

The thought still left a sinking feeling in her stomach. Cassidy felt like she was watching a missile head right toward the island, a missile that would cause certain destruction, but she was powerless to stop it. Powerless to evacuate people before the explosion hit. Powerless to use herself as a shield to protect others.

She closed her eyes and lifted a prayer for the safety of the residents here.

As soon as she muttered amen, she picked up the phone and tried to call Becky, Frankie's girlfriend. Becky didn't answer, so she left a message.

Out of curiosity, she ran a background check on Frankie. Most of what she read wasn't a surprise. But one fact toward the end of her search made her pause.

Frankie and his family were originally from Ohio.

Dane was from Cincinnati.

Was that a coincidence?

Maybe.

But Cassidy would need to check that out.

What if the two of them—Frankie and Dane— were working together? The idea seemed absurd. But that didn't mean it didn't have merit.

Fielding and Easton had just left the interrogation room.

It was time for Cassidy to go talk to Dane.

———

"I'M TELLING YOU, Cassidy, I have no idea how those items got into my trashcan." Dane raked a hand through his dark, thick hair. "You know me better than this."

Cassidy wanted to believe him, but she had more questions first.

Dane sat across from her in the interrogation room. He'd changed into jeans and a sweatshirt he kept in his locker at the station. The FBI had taken his cuffs off, but he looked like a different person as he sat in the dim room with its beige walls and stale smell. No police officer wanted to be on the other side of the table.

"Why did you choose to come to Lantern Beach, Dane?" Cassidy asked.

"I told you. I've always loved the beach. I wanted a small town. City life was draining me and making me feel burned out. Why are you asking?"

"I'm just wondering. You came here around two months ago—around the same time Gilead's Cove started to grow."

His eyes widened. "Wait, you think I'm affiliated with Gilead's Cove? That I came here because of them? Next thing, you're going to tell me is you think I'm working with Anthony Gilead."

Cassidy didn't deny it. "Cincinnati wasn't far from the area of West Virginia/Kentucky where Gilead recruited."

"I would never get behind that man." Dane's gaze grew steely. "He makes me sick to my stomach."

He said the words convincingly.

"Someone on the inside has been spilling information to him," Cassidy said. "It's someone in my inner circle."

"And you think it's me." His voice sounded dull with disbelief. "I don't know what to say. It sounds like your mind is made up, Chief."

She heard the hurt of feeling betrayed in his voice and winced.

"It's not made up, Dane," Cassidy said. "But I need to proceed carefully."

"I thought you would back me up."

"Dane, it's my job to be thorough and to ask questions. That's all I'm doing right now." She leaned closer. "And I have another question to ask you, one that I'm not sure you'll like."

"Go ahead."

"Someone saw you and Frankie Simpson nearly

get into a fight. What's your relationship with the man?"

"Frankie Simpson? The only time I talked to him was to warn him about how he treated his girlfriend. The two of us have nothing in common. Believe me."

"He's actually from Ohio also."

Dane shook his head. "So you think we're related or something?"

"Again, I'm just asking questions, and I still have a few more. They're questions that will probably make you uncomfortable."

"Ask me anything. I don't have anything to hide."

Cassidy licked her lips, unsure if she really wanted these answers but knowing she had to have them anyway. "Dane, I saw you give something to Anthony Gilead yesterday at the election site. What was it?"

His eyes narrowed. "You mean, out behind the school?"

"Yes." At least Dane didn't deny it.

"Gilead dropped his cell phone. I rushed out back to give it to him before he left."

That could be a plausible explanation. Cassidy would need to verify it, of course. "Any idea how your fingerprints ended up on the piping bag?"

"I have no idea. But it's not because I put

salmonella inside it so I could spread food poisoning throughout the town."

"Good to know."

Dane leaned forward. "Cassidy, I need your help. Don't let me go to jail for this. Please. You can check my records. Check my finances. Check whatever you want. But I didn't do this. I've been set up, and you have to figure out by who."

CHAPTER NINETEEN

CASSIDY KISSED Ty on the cheek after she stepped inside their cottage. Before she could say anything, Kujo and Ranger wandered over. She rubbed their heads and murmured a few greetings to the dogs.

As she looked up, Ty's friend came into view. The man was exactly as Ty had described him. Tall, thick, handsome. Looking at him, Cassidy couldn't even see the skin that had been grafted on his arm and shoulder after being injured by the IED.

"Colton Locke." She extended her hand. "I've heard a lot about you."

"And I've heard a lot about you. It's great to finally meet the woman who captured this guy's heart. I was beginning to wonder if he even had a heart buried down in there."

"Very funny," Ty said. "Don't listen to a word he

says."

"Oh, I want to hear everything he has to say. I'm sure you have some stories to tell."

"Oh, do I. Did Ty ever tell you about the time he rescued someone stranded on a boat surrounded by pirates near Somalia?"

Cassidy raised her eyebrows at her husband. "No, he didn't. After dinner, we're definitely talking. I want to hear more."

"He was practically G.I. Joe. He was always the guy who got the job done when you needed him."

"I can totally see where he got that reputation."

"Let me tell you, Ty was hanging by a rope from a helicopter, holding the woman he rescued. A reporter was embedded with us and took a picture of the scene. It was a silhouette with the sun setting in the distance—no personal details could be made out. That photo actually made the cover of *TIME* magazine."

Cassidy turned toward her husband. "I saw that magazine cover. It's practically iconic. You never told me about that."

Ty put his hands on Cassidy's shoulders and directed her away from Colton. "Maybe this was a bad idea."

"I think it's a great idea," Cassidy teased. "I love that I can learn new things about you."

Ty expertly changed the subject. "So, when are Melva and Mac getting here? You're not trying to fix them up or something, are you?"

"No, absolutely not. I could never see them together." Cassidy glanced at her watch. "And they're supposed to be here in fifteen minutes. I almost invited Leggott, but someone has to stay at the station with Dane. Leggott volunteered. Anyway, thanks for agreeing to this impromptu dinner."

"You know I like having people over. Though Melva was a surprising choice."

"The woman always seems afraid of me. And she doesn't feel like she has anyone here on the island. I know the timing is probably bad, but I started feeling like I should have made more of an effort to get to know her. She does work for me. I've had Dane and Leggott over to eat. For some reason, I never thought about Melva."

"She's a little peculiar," Ty said. "She always seems so nervous, and her eye contact leaves a lot to be desired."

"Yes, she is a little different, but even people who are different need friends, right?"

"Absolutely."

"Anyway, Melva has lived on the island for a while. It will be nice to get her insight on things around here. She's probably a resource I should have tapped into a long time ago. She's so quiet, I never really think about it."

"Well, Colton and I caught some red drum, so I'll have dinner ready to cook a little closer to the time everyone's here."

"Sounds great. Let me go change."

Cassidy hoped this break from the investigation would help her clear her head.

Quickly, she hopped into the shower and let the warm water wash over her. She tried to be excited about this dinner, but she wasn't. Honestly, she either wanted to work or spend time alone with Ty.

But she knew deep down inside that having Melva over would be good for all parties involved. She just needed a burst of energy she didn't seem to have.

———

"I SHOULD HAVE BROUGHT SOMETHING," Melva said, rubbing her hands together as she stepped into the cottage. "I didn't even think about it."

"Don't worry about it," Cassidy said, ushering her inside. "We've got it all taken care of."

"That's right," Mac called from the kitchen, where he stood with Ty. "I never bring anything. They're used to it."

"No, we're keeping a tab," Ty called. "But only for Mac."

"I guess I'm a little rusty when it comes to social situations," Melva continued, almost as if she didn't hear Mac and Ty. "It's usually just me and my cats."

Cassidy watched as Kujo and Ranger came over and sniffed Melva's feet. "I think the dogs know you prefer felines."

"Those cats are my babies. I've got six of them." She looked down at the dogs and took a step back, almost looking fearful.

"Kujo, Ranger, get back." Cassidy pulled out a seat at the table and waited until Melva lowered herself there before sitting beside her. "Six cats, huh?"

"They're all I have," Melva said.

"I know we've worked together for a while, but I don't know much about your family. You said you have a daughter and granddaughter?"

"That's right. They live out in California. Moved there for my son-in-law's job. I haven't seen them in two years now."

"I guess they don't get out to visit much." Ty called from the kitchen while tossing the salad.

"No, they have their own lives. Whenever they do have days off from work, they like to take vacations where they can relax. Can't blame them." Melva might have tried to sound convincing, but a deep frown tugged at her lips.

"You should go and visit them sometime," Cassidy said. "You have plenty of days off banked."

Mac joined them at the table.

"I have to admit I hate traveling." Melva pushed her glasses up and glanced around nervously. "I've lived on this island for twenty years, you know."

Ty set a salad in front of everyone and encouraged his guests to dig in.

"Is that right?" Cassidy asked. "I had no idea you were such a local, Melva. There's so much I don't know about you."

Melva picked up her fork. "Oh, yes. I used to live out by where the ferry docks are now."

"There are no houses out that way," Cassidy said.

"But there used to be," Mac said. "The ferry docks used to be located a half mile down the road, but the water channels changed, and the transportation system was having to dredge constantly. They finally moved the ferry terminal to its current location."

"I never knew that," Cassidy said. "I still have so much to learn about this island."

"Yes, they sure did." Melva offered a tight smile. "The government tore down all those old houses and built what we currently have today. They called it progress."

"Hopefully, they paid you well," Mac muttered. "Emminent domain and all."

She shrugged. "You know how those things go."

"I don't think I've ever asked this question before," Cassidy continued. "But who hired you, Melva? Was it Mac or Bozeman?"

"Bozeman," Melva said. "I've worked for the police department for five years now. The job kind of dropped into my lap. After I married, I was a homemaker. When my daughter started school, I joined the work force again. I was a clerk at the general store when Bozeman hired me."

"Did he hire you out of the blue?" Ty asked. "That's a big jump."

"He and my husband were friends, so I think that's how it came about." Melva shrugged. "Anyway, enough about me. Thank you again for having me over."

"I'm just sorry we weren't able to do it sooner," Cassidy said before taking a bite of her salad.

"Being single and older, it's easy to be overlooked. I don't mean to complain. It just hits me more in the winter."

As soon as they finished their salads, Ty served the rest of dinner, and they dug into their fish, rice, and asparagus. Several bites in, Melva cleared her throat.

"Do you really believe Dane is behind this food poisoning?" Melva's gaze latched onto Cassidy's.

Cassidy exchanged a glance with the rest of the gang. "It's hard to say. We have to let the investigation run its course and give it due process. I don't want to believe it."

Melva lowered her fork. "I guess the feds are in charge now?"

Cassidy nodded. "That's right. This case is bigger than our island. The person responsible for making all these people sick is going to face some hefty charges."

"I heard it was bioterrorism." Melva shook her head. "I never thought I'd see the day when that happened here on Lantern Beach."

"You and me both," Mac said.

"Like I said, the charges are serious. A lot of people got sick. One person died." Cassidy leaned back as the details settled in her mind again. "What do you think about this case, Melva?"

Her fork remained lowered, and surprise ran over her features. "Me? I don't know what to think. Never seen anything like it. I thought salmonella was something that started on farms, not that it was something people could grow themselves."

"It's true," Cassidy said. "You can order it online."

"And then you have to grow it?" Melva squinted, as if trying to process everything.

Cassidy nodded. "That's right. It's quite the process, but way easier to do than it should be."

Melva shook her head. "Well, I just think that's a shame. You can't trust anyone anymore, can you?"

"No, you can't," Mac said. "And it is sad."

As if on cue, Cassidy's phone buzzed. She excused herself for a moment to check the message.

It was a report she'd requested containing Dane's phone records. She wanted to see who he'd been talking to lately.

She quickly scanned the list.

One number caught her eye.

Cassidy didn't know who it belonged to. But she did know it was the same number she'd gotten some of her threatening text messages from.

It was looking more and more like Dane was indeed their guy.

———

AFTER DINNER, which had been delicious, they had dessert and coffee, all prepared by Ty. His hot fudge sundae was tasty, and Cassidy was grateful she had a husband who didn't mind cooking.

Melva had left, Colton had retired to his cabana to

rest, and Cassidy was grateful to have some time to talk to Ty and Mac, two of her most trusted confidants. The night had been a success, though. Melva had seemed more comfortable. She'd even pitched in to help, fetching coffee refills and offering to help do the dishes.

Now Cassidy was ready to let down her guard.

"How are you holding up?" Mac asked her, a fatherly look about him as he gazed at her with concern in his eyes.

"Maybe I should ask you that question." Cassidy missed Mac's quirky side. The side of him that scaled the side of his house to keep up with his SWAT skills. The side of him that trained search and rescue dogs and organized mini-police academies for kids on spring break.

Mac shrugged, a faraway look in his gaze. "I don't know what to think. Of course, I'm disappointed about the election, but I'm not ready to give up the fight yet."

"No one here on the island is," Ty said. "We just can't believe that Gilead won."

"Well, he did. And now we have to deal with the repercussions. But enough about the election for now." Mac leaned forward. "You get any more of those threatening texts lately, Cassidy?"

She frowned. "No, I haven't. I'm kind of surprised. I got five, and now it's nothing."

Mac grunted. "Strange."

Cassidy picked up her cup of tea and let the steam hit her face. "That's what I thought too. Why stop?"

"Maybe they got distracted," Ty said as he sat down beside her, resting his arm on the couch behind Cassidy. His voice turned dry as he shrugged. "Maybe the texter got caught in the middle of . . . oh, I don't know . . . an election or something."

Mac raised an eyebrow. "You still think Gilead is behind the texts?"

Ty shrugged. "I don't know. But the timeline would fit. He was away on his honeymoon, after all."

Cassidy shifted and put her drink on the coffee table. Tension embedded itself in her shoulders as she braced herself to share the news. "There's something I need to tell you both. Whoever sent those texts to me . . . their number was found in Dane's phone."

"What?" Ty's body went from easygoing to uptight in the blink of an eye.

Cassidy nodded. "It's true. I just got his records and looked at them. I didn't want to say anything while we were eating."

Mac shook his head and rubbed his chin, his eyes

closing in disappointment. "So Dane really might be tied to all of this."

"I don't want to believe it," Cassidy said. "I really don't."

"But assumptions are your enemy," Ty reminded her.

"Yes, they are," she agreed.

"How would Dane have found out about your past?"

"If Dane is behind this, there's obviously a lot more to him than any of us assumed. There are intersections in my past—in your past, Ty—to what's going on here. I don't know what. And I don't like it."

"I don't like it either," Ty said. "In fact, I'm really glad Dane is locked up right now because otherwise I'd be tempted to pay him a visit. He's put your life on the line."

Cassidy leaned back. "Was it like this when you were police chief here, Mac?"

He snorted. "No, not at all. We gave out speeding tickets. Broke up brawls. Had a few domestic disputes. I'm not sure what's going on here on the island."

"It seems to be happening only since I came." Did she bring trouble with her? Because she just couldn't catch a break.

"Things come in squalls, Cassidy." Mac's voice sounded quiet with wisdom. "You didn't bring trouble here."

"But I did. DH-7 followed me here."

"And the blame for that is purely on DH-7," Ty added.

"Now there's Gilead's Cove," Cassidy reminded them.

Mac tilted his head with doubt. "Certainly you don't blame yourself for that also."

"I don't blame myself. I just . . . I don't know. It's been a storm of crime, and I don't feel like I have the power to stop it." Cassidy didn't like to voice her doubts aloud. She wanted to be positive and resilient. But everything was starting to wear her down.

"You don't have the power to stop it." Ty's firm hand covered her knee, bringing her back to reality, as did his sturdy, confident voice. "You simply find the people who are responsible."

"After all, people will realize that you mean business," Mac added. "They won't want to come here to start trouble."

"You really think so?" Cassidy asked.

Mac nodded. "Yeah, really. Trust me on this one."

"I'll try to." But her old life in Seattle was starting to seem like a walk in the park compared to the problems here in Lantern Beach.

CHAPTER TWENTY

MORIAH PLUCKED her eyes open from a deep sleep. As she did, some kind of internal alarm filled her. Her breaths came rapidly. Her lungs squeezed. Panic wanted to choke her.

What . . .?

Had she been having a bad dream? That must be it, even though she couldn't remember any details. Why else would she be feeling so much panic for no apparent reason?

Taking in a deep breath to try and slow her heartbeat, her eyes traveled to the other side of the bed. It was empty.

Gilead must have already gotten up and let Moriah sleep in.

Her panic subsided even more and relief filled her. She would have a few minutes to herself before she started her day. It wasn't that she didn't love her husband. But he could be overbearing, and some time alone sounded really refreshing. She'd barely had a moment since they'd gotten married.

Lazily, she stretched her arms and legs across the covers, reveling in having room to breathe. Her knees and hands still hurt from scrubbing the bedroom yesterday. She hated manual labor. Hated it. But, in the end, Gilead had given his stamp of approval. He'd even drawn a warm bath for her as a reward. It almost made it all worth it.

This would be worth it, she reminded herself. Though the start of her marriage felt rocky, once things evened out, she would feel like royalty. She'd be esteemed and admired here in the community. Maybe she'd even be given some freedom.

She smiled at the thought.

Maybe one day she'd ask Gilead about that life insurance policy. She just needed to gain a little more trust with him.

As Moriah turned over in bed, she let out a gasp.

Gilead . . .

He sat in the chair beside her bed, facing her backside, silently watching her.

"Gi . . . Gilead," she stuttered, pulling herself upright. "I didn't know you were there. How long have you been watching me?"

He smiled, but the gesture looked empty. "About an hour."

"You should have woken me."

"But you look so angelic when you sleep."

She pulled the covers tighter, a sinking feeling echoing in her stomach. "Do I?"

"It's quite a contrast to when you're awake." His smile slipped.

Something about his tone caused fear to slice through her. "What . . . what do you mean?"

"It means that you're not so angelic when I'm not watching you, Moriah." His voice came out as a low growl.

She drew back, another shot of panic sending pulses through her. Her mind raced. What was he referring to?

"I don't know what you're talking about. I would never do anything against your wishes."

He reached down and pulled up something from the floor. It was a clear plastic bag full of . . . bread.

The blood drained from her face as she feared what might happen next. "How'd you find that?"

"It was in your drawer."

Gilead had gone through her drawers. More panic rose. Moriah had carefully hidden the bag in a tunic so it couldn't be easily discovered. She'd thought she was in the clear—but Gilead had obviously been thorough. Terrifyingly thorough.

"Gilead, you know I have hypoglycemia," she started. "I have to eat for my health, and it's not always on the same schedule that meals are served here."

His gaze darkened. "You need to trust that God will take care of these things."

"I do. But He gave me food so that I could eat when I feel bad and—"

"I'll be the judge of that." Gilead's voice took on a hard edge that matched his gaze. Gone was the warm, affable leader everyone admired. A monster took his place. "Do you understand?"

Moriah scooted back again, pressing herself into the wooden headboard and wishing she could disappear. "I didn't do it to disobey you. It's just that—"

Gilead sliced his hand through the air. "But you did disobey me. And that's one of the only things I asked for. Obedience and respect. That's all every husband here asks for. I thought you understood that."

"I do, Gilead. I do. I'm sorry. I shouldn't have taken the bread." Desperation caused her voice to crack.

"No, you shouldn't have."

She held her breath, wondering if Gilead was

going to let this go. If he would let her off with just a reprimand.

Please. Please!

He stood, dropping the bread to the floor. "Get out of bed, Moriah."

Her legs felt wobbly as she stood, but Moriah didn't dare defy him. Her nightgown fell above her knees, and she straightened it, trying to carefully think through anything that might make her husband angry.

"Come with me," he ordered, stepping toward the door.

"Can I get dressed first?"

"No, come as you are."

"But—"

He swirled around, fire still in his gaze. "Are you arguing with me?"

Guilt pounded at her. "No, sir."

Obediently, she fell into step behind him. Moriah followed him out the bedroom door and into the hallway. Self-consciously, she touched her hair, wishing she'd had time to make herself more presentable, to put on something more decent.

Horror rose in her when she saw Gilead walking down the stairs.

Gilead was going to make her go out like this in public?

Why would Gilead do this? Why wouldn't he protect Moriah's modesty?

Moriah knew better than to argue with him. She'd already poked the bear, so to speak, more than once.

Heat rose on her cheeks as they stepped into the cafeteria. Everyone was already there, eating silently at the tables that had been set up in rows across the room. Their gazes rose and burned into her as she followed her husband through the Meeting Place.

She expected him to parade her onstage. But, to her surprise, he didn't. Instead, he led her outside.

A cool, early morning wind swept over the landscape, going right through her thin nightgown. Gilead's hand grabbed hers with a vise-like grip, and he kept walking.

Where in the world was he taking her? Dread pooled in her stomach.

They walked toward the beach, an area where the sandy shore met the Pamlico Sound. But that didn't make sense.

A cry lodged in Moriah's throat. She halfway wanted to yell for help. She halfway wished she'd taken the police chief up on her offer to rescue her. But she hadn't, and now she had to live with those choices.

Gilead led her toward a fence, pushed some vines aside, and opened a gate there. They stepped into the woods that surrounded the south side of the compound.

They were leaving.

Moriah sucked in a breath.

But why?

"Gilead—" She tried to slow her steps so they could talk.

"It isn't your place to ask questions," he snapped. "I need silence."

Moriah could hardly breathe as worst-case scenarios fluttered through her mind.

Was her husband going to kill her out here? Bury her body?

No, Gilead wouldn't do that . . . right? Moriah wished she felt more certain.

But if he did murder her—who would notice she was missing? Who would call the police?

No one, Moriah realized. No one would go against Gilead.

Five minutes into their trek through the woods, Gilead stopped in the middle of nowhere. What was he doing?

Moriah's breaths came shallow and quick. Her feet hurt from walking barefoot, and she could feel the scrapes against her legs. And the chill she felt was painful. The cool air crept up her nightgown, and no part of her was truly protected from the elements.

He reached down, through the tangled under-brush, and, a moment later, he jerked his arm up. A door opened.

A door? What was a door doing on the forest floor?

A dank smell drifted upward from the dark abyss hidden amongst the wildlife.

It almost looked like . . . an old bunker.

"Inside," Gilead directed.

Moriah knew she couldn't fight him, even if she wanted. He would overpower her. She might as well try to make this easy.

On the verge of a panic attack, Moriah crept onto the first step. And then the next. And the next. Gilead remained right behind her, ensuring she couldn't run.

When she hit the last step, suffocating darkness surrounded her. Gilead fiddled with something, and light filled the room. An old lantern, she realized. He kept an old gas lantern down here. Or had it been left over from times past? It didn't matter right now.

She glanced around the space with cement walls and spiderwebs and collections of crisp, dried leaves that huddled in fear against walls and in corners. But it was the newer items that had been placed here that made her head spin.

Handcuffs attached to a wall. A poker. A . . . whip?

"No . . ." The word came out as the air left her lungs. Reality hit her, and it hit her hard.

Moriah tried to back up, but Gilead caught her waist and jostled her forward.

She dug her heels into the ground, trying to use her body weight to prevent whatever was about to happen. When that didn't work, she thrashed her arms out.

But it was no use. Gilead was bigger and stronger than she was.

He twirled her around and let out a soft shush. For a moment—and just a moment—her frantic heart slowed. Maybe this wasn't what she thought it was. Gilead didn't look angry. He looked calm. Maybe too calm.

"Moriah, my love." One of Gilead's hands stroked her face while the other gripped her hard enough to ensure she wouldn't run. "You know how much you mean to me."

"Yes." Her voice quivered with doubt.

His gaze softened along with his voice. "Love can be so hard sometimes. Becoming the person we were meant to be is often a road forged by fire."

She said nothing. Just waited.

Gilead stroked his hand across her face again, his

eyes warm with what resembled affection. "You are the person God told me to marry, and I know we're meant to be together."

Then get me out of here. She kept the words silent out of fear of angering Gilead. She would hear him out. Maybe this wasn't as bad as she'd thought. Maybe she was just paranoid.

"But I need you to be the person worthy of leading this group," he murmured. "We don't have time for you to ease into this new role, especially now that I'm mayor. Do you understand?"

She clung to him, fearful of what might happen next. "I don't know."

Gilead leaned closer, close enough that his breath hit her cheek. "I just need you to learn to be obedient."

"But I am—"

He placed his finger over Moriah's mouth before raking his hand through her hair. It snagged on a tangle, but that didn't stop him. He kept pushing his fingers until she whimpered in pain.

"No, you're not, Moriah," he whispered. "I didn't want to do this the hard way."

"You don't have to. I won't mess up again. I promise." Her head swam, and she feared she might pass out from anxiety.

"I know you won't mess up again. We can't afford for you to do that."

Moriah clung to her husband, desperate to get through, to convince him she could be the wife he needed, that he desired. "I'll do whatever you say. I promise."

"That ship has already sailed, dear. Now we have to attend the school of hard knocks. You're familiar with it, aren't you?"

He knew about her past. She'd never told him about all the trouble she'd been in. "Gilead—"

"Yes?"

At his tone, her hopes of changing his mind shriveled to nothing. "What are you going to do?"

"I'm going to give you some time to think."

Fear lodged in her throat. "Here?"

He took her wrist and kissed it gently. Then, without letting go, he raised her arm and backed up.

"No, no, no!" The realization of what Gilead was doing swept over Moriah until she felt lightheaded.

"It's going to be okay. I promise."

"Please, don't do this to me. Please." Tears streamed down her face.

One of the shackles clicked on her wrist, trapping her against the dank wall filled with bugs and spider webs. Filled with moisture and filth. Cold seeped through her nightgown, and the darkness closed in even tighter.

"It's for your best." Gilead swept a hair out of her eyes. "You'll see."

For a moment, he looked like he might kiss her. His face lingered close. His gaze took on a hungry look.

Instead, he backed up, nodded, and waved.

He was leaving her.

A scream emerged from Moriah's depths as full-fledged panic captured her muscles. She thrashed against her shackle, tried to reach for Gilead, tried to fight with everything in her to stop this from happening.

But, in the blink of an eye, the daylight disappeared, and a pit of blackness—a pit that matched her despair—enveloped her.

A terror like she'd never felt before consumed her. All she could think about was that death seemed like a better alternative to this new life she'd thought would be so perfect.

CHAPTER TWENTY-ONE

CASSIDY SAT UP IN BED, unsure what had awakened her. Early morning gray filled the room, and she glanced beside her at Ty.

Her husband lay in a ball holding his stomach, and a slight moan escaped from him.

She bent toward him and gripped his arm with concern. "Ty?"

His eyes squeezed together, but he didn't otherwise move. "I'm not feeling great, Cass."

"Your stomach?"

"Yes." His voice sounded strained. "I feel clammy. Nauseated."

Pieces connected in her mind—pieces she didn't like, but that she knew fit. "Could the food poisoning be hitting you this late?"

"I have no idea." He let out another soft groan,

and Kujo rose from the floor, walking over to check on his owner.

Cassidy jumped out of bed and grabbed some clothes to get dressed. "I should get you to the clinic."

Ty shook his hand in the air, motioning for her to stop. "I'll be fine, Cassidy. I'm otherwise healthy. I just need to let this run its course."

"But—" She couldn't stand seeing her normally tough husband in so much pain.

"The clinic is already slammed. There's no reason for me to go. I don't need fluids or anything. I'll be okay."

Cassidy frowned, desperately wishing she could do something to make him feel better. But there was nothing. If this was food poisoning, Ty was right. It would need to run its course.

She continued getting dressed in her police uniform, knowing she needed to get moving anyway. Sleep was long forgotten at this point.

"Why is yours hitting so late, Ty?" Cassidy muttered, not expecting Ty to answer. "Is there another outbreak of this?"

"I don't know."

"What did you eat that I didn't?"

He let out another low moan as he turned over. His face looked pale and his eyes listless. "I really don't know. I did grab a sandwich at The Docks yesterday at lunchtime."

The Docks was a waterfront restaurant located in the boardwalk area of the island. It boasted outdoor seating and expensive meals.

"I'm going to need to check that out, then." But a bad feeling lingered in her gut. What if this food poisoning incident was happening all over again? And, if that was the case, Dane couldn't be responsible this time. He'd been locked up.

The questions circled Cassidy's mind.

"You go to work, Cassidy." Ty grabbed her hand and squeezed it, as if commissioning her to leave. "Figure out who did this. That's the best way you can help me."

With a new sense of dread—and determination—in her stomach, Cassidy nodded. "Okay. I will. But you call me if you need me. Promise me."

"I will."

"I love you, Ty." She kissed his forehead.

"I love you too, Cass."

———

ON HER WAY out the door, Cassidy called Clemson. No other cases of food poisoning had been reported, according to him. Not yet, at least.

"Clemson, could this be left over from the incident at Lisa's?" Cassidy asked, marveling at the brilliant colors of the sunrise on the horizon. Even in the midst of trouble and uncertainty, there was always something to be grateful for. Right now, it was the masterpiece all around her.

"I think that would be unusual for Ty's illness to manifest so late," Clemson said. "It is possible, however. Or this sickness could be unrelated. It seems unlikely, but I've seen crazier things happen."

Just as Cassidy expected, it was too early to know anything. "I'm going to go talk to Leo at The Docks, just to make sure we don't have another case of bioterrorism on our hands. I'll call Fielding and Easton from the FBI as well. They'll need to know about this."

"Do that, Cassidy. And I really hope this isn't a case of more food poisoning. I don't know if this island can take much more."

Cassidy didn't know either. And she didn't like it.

She ended the call and contacted Fielding and Easton, just as she'd said. They promised to meet her at Leo's house.

Leo Romano owned The Docks. He was a retired chef from New York, and his restaurant offered the standard island fare. He had a big business mind-set, much more so than Lisa's labor-of-love philosophy.

Cassidy had met Leo a few times, and he seemed nice enough. He was active in charity work on the island, but he did have more of a standoffish attitude that seemed to perfectly fit his Northeastern accent. In fact, when Cassidy had first met the man, she'd joked that he seemed like a member of the mob with his dark hair and affinity for cigars.

And the man had been at Mac's party. She'd be wise to keep that in mind also.

She pulled up to his home. It was a moderately-sized house two blocks from the ocean. With its dark-blue siding and clean white trim, the place appeared to be one of the newer structures on an island filled with mostly weathered, more rustic houses.

Once Fielding and Easton arrived, they knocked on Leo's door. He still wore a bathrobe, and he had a cup of coffee in hand. The man, in his early sixties, had his hair slicked back, and his prominent nose was red, like he had a cold or allergies.

"What brings you out so early?" he asked, his suspicious gaze darting between them. He remained inside his house, leaving the rest of them on the deck with the sun beating down.

"We need to ask you some questions about your menu yesterday," Fielding said.

Leo's face paled. "I really hope the conclusions I'm drawing are incorrect."

"So do we," Fielding said. "But someone who ate at The Docks yesterday is sick today. We don't know if it's because they ate at your restaurant, but we need to ask you some questions, just in case."

Leo began pacing just inside his doorway and muttering under his breath in what sounded like Italian.

"Was there anyone strange working there yesterday?" Cassidy asked, slipping her sunglasses on. The sun came over the roof of the house at just the right angle to nearly blind her.

"No, no one."

"You didn't offer any buffets?" Easton added.

"No, never. Buffets are only for second-class establishments."

"Was the food in your kitchen ever unsupervised?" Fielding continued, sounding all business.

Leo stopped pacing and put his coffee down. "No, the kitchen staff are the only ones who have access to the food. The people who work for me are family. None of them would do anything. This business is our livelihood." Emotion marked each of Leo's words, leaving little room for doubt. Whether he was correct or not remained to be seen, but he truly believed his words.

"Have you had any other reports of people becoming ill after eating here?" Cassidy asked.

"No, not at all," Leo said. "It was slow yesterday. We usually don't open this early in the season, but we decided to slowly introduce ourselves back to the community. It helps us all to get back into the swing of things before the tourists come."

"We're going to need to talk to your family and make sure they didn't see anything," Fielding said.

"I'll go get them." Leo frowned. "But I really hope this isn't what I think it is."

"So do I," Cassidy told him. "And I'm going to need to know if anyone out of the ordinary came into the restaurant yesterday."

Leo's eyes narrowed with thought. "Only one person I can think of off the top of my head."

"Who's that?" Cassidy asked, her breath catching with anticipation.

"That man with the NCSBI. I forget his name. But he said The Docks was his favorite, and he couldn't wait to get back and have some of our crab cakes."

The blood left Cassidy's face as conclusions she didn't want to draw formed a picture in her mind. "Agent Abbott?"

Leo snapped his fingers. "Yeah, that's him. He came back and sat at his favorite table by the water."

Why would Agent Abbott be back in Lantern Beach and not even tell Cassidy he was in town . . . unless he was involved in some way?

It was worth looking into. Because Abbott definitely seemed to have his own agenda and a strong dislike for Cassidy. She'd tried to dismiss it as simply a professional conflict . . . but what if there was more to it? What if Abbott was the one behind these incidents somehow?

That's what Cassidy needed to find out.

CHAPTER TWENTY-TWO

CASSIDY, Fielding, and Easton talked to the six members of Leo's family. No one had seen anything strange. They all confirmed it had been a slow day yesterday. They were even able to list most of the people who'd come in—because the majority had been locals.

Back in her car, Cassidy had called Doc Clemson once more. No other people had come in ill. Fielding and Easton had agreed they would wait and see if anyone else got sick before calling the health department or opening an official investigation.

Cassidy also called Ty, and he said he felt the same. He also promised that, if he got worse, he would go to the clinic or call Clemson.

In the meantime, Cassidy went back to the police

station. She needed to talk to Dane again and to figure out what Abbott was up to.

"Good morning, Cassidy," Melva called from behind the front desk.

Cassidy didn't even try to smile or pretend everything was great as she paused by Melva. She set some coffee and donuts on the counter. "Good morning, Melva."

The woman wrung her hands together, not appearing any less anxious than usual. Maybe they hadn't made any strides at dinner after all. "Thanks again for having me over last night. It was really nice."

"You're welcome. I'm glad you could come."

Melva squinted at Cassidy and absently straightened a jar of pens on the front desk. "Everything okay?"

"Ty isn't feeling well," Cassidy admitted. "I wonder if it's food poisoning."

Melva frowned, sticking the final pen into the jar before looking back at Cassidy. "Oh, no. I heard that Gertie wasn't feeling well either. She ate at The Docks yesterday. Not sure if that's related or not. She was also at Mac's party."

"Gertie?" Gertie was a pet groomer here on the island. Though she was into her seventies, the woman loved her job so much that she said she wouldn't stop until she died. The woman was a force to be reckoned with, for sure.

"That's right. I ran into her husband this morning when I stopped to get gas. He told me she got sick last night."

"She has symptoms of food poisoning?" Cassidy asked, thinking maybe there was more to The Docks connection than she wanted to believe.

Melva shrugged. "Same as everyone else, I suppose. I didn't ask for a lot of details."

"That's good to know. Thanks, Melva. We'll follow up on that."

Grabbing her coffee and donuts, Cassidy bypassed her office and headed down the opposite hallway toward the holding cell area. She hadn't been able to stop thinking about seeing that familiar phone number on Dane's records. What exactly was his connection to the person who'd sent Cassidy those threats?

She intended to find out.

But as she spotted Dane, she paused.

Dane sat up on the stiff bed, his head lowered and shoulders drooped. He looked totally beaten down, so much so that Cassidy's heart panged with empathy. The man looked devastated by this turn of events.

"Hey," she called, keeping her voice even.

Traditional training would tell her to pounce and try to find answers. But Cassidy's gut told her she needed to tread gently and that Dane, despite what he had or hadn't done, needed some grace right now.

Dane looked up. When he spotted Cassidy, he strode toward the bars, a vague glimmer of hope returning to his eyes. "Did you find out anything?"

"You know I can't tell you that." She handed him a package of powdered donuts and some coffee from the general store. She'd picked them up just for Dane. "But I did bring you this. Thought you could be hungry."

He looked less than enthused as he took it from her, but he did take a sip of his coffee. As he pulled the cup away from his mouth, Dane stared at her with enough intensity to make Cassidy shift with unease.

"What can you tell me?" Dane asked.

"Very little."

"Are you still investigating, at least?"

"I am. I want to find the truth, Dane."

He leaned closer to the bars, his eyes nearly bulging. "Then you need to keep looking. Because I didn't do this, Cassidy."

Cassidy swallowed hard and reminded herself to stay objective, to keep her emotions out of this case.

It was easier said than done. "Did you think of anything else that might help your case, Dane?"

He shrugged and took another sip of his coffee. "No, I've been thinking about it all night. But there's nothing. I wish there was."

She pulled a piece of paper from her pocket and handed it to him. "Whose number is this?"

Dane stared at the paper a moment before shaking his head. "I have no idea. Why?"

"It was listed on your phone records. You received a call from that number about a week ago."

He glanced up at her, a hard look in his eyes. "I'm assuming this is relevant to the investigation?"

Cassidy said nothing.

"Look, I don't recognize the number. Just because someone called me doesn't mean I talked to them. It could have been a wrong number. How long was the conversation?"

"About thirty seconds."

"That could have just been me saying hello over and over again. I have no idea. I really don't."

"Good to know." Cassidy wanted to believe him. She really did. But she'd be naïve to simply take his word, especially considering her life was on the line.

Dane's gaze locked with hers. "Keep looking, Cassidy. Please."

She nodded as she stepped back. "I'm going to

get back to work now. But I will keep looking Dane. I'll keep searching until I find the truth."

———

SITTING AT HER DESK, Cassidy passed on the message about Gertie to Fielding and Easton, who promised to look into it. Afterward, she tried to call Frankie's girlfriend, Becky, again. Still no answer. Her last call was to Agent Abbott. He also didn't answer.

Lowering her phone back to her desk, Cassidy let out a long breath.

When is this going to end, Lord?

Her problems seemed to keep going on and on with no end in sight. She couldn't catch a break, and neither could the island. While she didn't want to feel sorry for herself, she was exhausted.

Cassidy's mind drifted over everything that had happened, from Gilead's Cove moving into town, to the threatening text messages she'd received recently, to her friend Serena going off to join the cult.

In the past month, a dead man had washed ashore. Three bodies had been found in the woods. A trio of dangerous criminals had robbed a general store and abducted Cassidy.

Maybe when she'd taken this job, she'd bitten off more than she could chew.

Cassidy hardly ever wanted to give in to doubt whenever the emotion reared its head. But maybe it was time to take a hard look at herself.

She sighed and took another sip of her coffee, which was getting cold. She didn't even care at the moment.

She had a long list of things to do right now. But instead of starting at the top, she picked up her phone one more time. She tried again to call Rhonda, Gilead's first wife. Cassidy had tried several times before, but the woman never picked up her phone.

This time it rang and rang.

On the sixth ring, someone actually answered.

"Hello?" a jolting male voice said.

Cassidy sat up straighter. Maybe things were looking up today after all. "Good morning, I'm Police Chief Cassidy Chambers of Lantern Beach, North Carolina. I'm trying to reach Rhonda Becker."

"There's no Rhonda Becker here."

Cassidy nibbled the inside of her lip. This was the last address Rhonda Becker had listed on her tax return and one of her credit cards had been linked to this location as well. "Are you certain? It's important that we find her."

"The woman who was living here just disappeared a few weeks ago without any explanation. She left some money that covered a month's rent and a note saying she needed to move on. And then she was gone. Now I'm trying to get it ready for another tenant."

The news washed over Cassidy and excitement bubbled inside her. Maybe she was finally closing in on some answers. "What did she look like?"

"She was probably in her mid-twenties," the man said, his accent distinctly New Jersey. "Blonde hair. Thin build. Kind of quiet. What else do you want to know?"

The picture Cassidy had seen of Rhonda had shown a brunette with haunted eyes and an unconvincing smile. Her hair had been long and unstyled, and her skin pale but flawless.

Cassidy knew what it was like to go into hiding and try to start a new life. She'd had the FBI assisting her when she'd done so. Someone who didn't have that advantage might have to use an old credit card. Might not know how to officially get a new identity.

Most people trying to hide from their past changed their names. Their hair color and cut. The way they dressed.

Cassidy felt certain the woman staying at this apartment had been Rhonda. And she'd fled. Maybe she'd feared that Anthony Gilead had found her, and she'd gone into hiding again.

She thanked the landlord and leaned back in her seat.

How was she going to find someone who wanted to disappear? Perhaps she needed to examine her own life to find those answers.

Before Cassidy could dwell on it too long, her phone rang. It was Niles Shepherd.

"Hi, Niles."

"Hey, Chief Chambers. Listen, I'm not one for gossip, but I don't like what's happening here on the island any more than anyone else. That's why I'm telling you this."

"Telling me what?" Her curiosity spiked.

"Three nights ago, I saw Rebecca Jarvis having dinner with a man I'd never seen before," he blurted.

"Not her husband?"

"No, definitely not her husband. This man wore a tunic."

"Kind of like the people at Gilead's Cove . . ." Her breath caught.

"Exactly. Anyway, I was trying not to rush to judgment or anything. But I just heard this morning that Rebecca's husband left her."

"What?" She'd just talked to Rebecca yesterday . . .

"That was the scuttlebutt down at the . . . the party I went to this morning."

"The party? This morning?"

He paused. "Okay, so it actually wasn't a party. It was my breakfast book club. Don't judge me."

"I'm not." Cassidy smiled. Niles always amused her, though rarely on purpose. "Go ahead."

"One of the ladies runs into Jim at the pier every morning, bright and early. He likes to fish in his free time, especially since he lost his job. He wasn't there today, so people started to talk. I thought you should know, especially since I know Rebecca sold her property to Gilead's Cove. I don't know what's going on but 'see something, say something,' right?"

"Thanks, Niles."

"Catch whoever did this, Chief."

"I'm trying. I really am trying."

CASSIDY DECIDED to pay another visit to Rebecca Jarvis. When the woman opened the door, her eyes were red-rimmed, and she looked like she hadn't slept in days. The drastic change had happened quickly.

Rebecca didn't say anything when she spotted Cassidy. She simply pulled the door open, stepped aside, and allowed Cassidy to come in. Silently, Cassidy took a seat across from her on the couch.

Cassidy quickly noted the balls of tissues everywhere. The laundry piling up in a basket in the corner. A plate with dried egg yolk sat on the coffee table.

This definitely wasn't up to Rebecca's usually tidy standards.

"How are you doing, Rebecca?" Cassidy asked, keeping her tone gentle.

She'd come here with the intentions of grilling the woman, but she couldn't do that right now. No, there was something else going on that Cassidy wanted to be sensitive to.

"I've been better." Rebecca sniffled and pressed a tissue under her nose. "I know why you're here."

"Why's that?"

"You heard that Jim left me. You probably think it's because of this real estate deal or because he discovered I've secretly joined Gilead's Cove or something."

Unfortunately, Rebecca was correct. "Is that true?"

Alarm filled the woman's gaze, as if she'd expected Cassidy to think her words were a joke. "Of course not. I told you we've been tight on money since Jim lost his job. That's the only reason I sold that property."

"Someone saw you meeting with a member of

Gilead's Cove a few days ago." Cassidy decided just to lay it out there.

Rebecca seemed unfazed by the observation, like her emotions had run their course and she had little left to react with now. "I did. But it was about the real estate deal, no other reason."

Cassidy drew in a deep breath before asking her next question. "Rebecca, I hate to bring this up, but what happened between you and your husband exactly?"

Rebecca sniffled again, but her shoulders seemed to sag even more than before. "Just financial problems. It's a lot of stress on a marriage."

"What did your husband do, Rebecca?" Cassidy had seen Jim from a distance, but she'd never talked to the man. He hadn't seemed especially outgoing or friendly.

"He worked for one of the local management companies. Last year, his boss thought Jim took some money from the business. But he didn't. He wouldn't do that."

"Did his boss press charges?"

Rebecca shook her head, a far-off look in her eyes. "No, he didn't. He said he didn't want to take it that far. This was before you came here and took over as police chief. But no one else wants to hire Jim now because rumor got out about what happened. No one wants to hire a thief."

"Why did his boss think Jim stole money from the company?"

Rebecca shrugged, resting a hand at her throat and closing her eyes as if to squeeze out her emotion. "The funds disappeared, but it was just bad accounting. The whole thing wasn't Jim's fault. But once your reputation is ruined, it's ruined. It doesn't matter what the truth is."

"I see." Cassidy studied Rebecca's face—the strain there. The stress. She looked thinner, even though it had been only a day since she'd seen her. "Rebecca, why did Jim leave yesterday? What happened?"

Rebecca sniffled again and a noise escaped from her throat, a sound like a deep sob being suppressed —temporarily, at least. "He said I've been acting erratic lately."

"Have you?"

Rebecca shrugged, then nodded, then shrugged again. "Yeah, I guess I have. I mean, this is a slow time on the island workwise. Not many people are buying houses. Then we don't have his job to supplement our income. We had to go to the food pantry once. It was humbling, to say the least."

"So what happened before he left?"

Rebecca's chin trembled. "I got an angry phone call last night from one of the locals who thought I'd sold out to Gilead's Cove. He said he would tell everyone what I'd done, and that no one would ever want to use me as a realtor in this area again."

"Who was this?"

Rebecca frowned, still staring in the distance as if reliving bad memories. "Matthias Williams at the general store. His wife was ill from the food poisoning. Everyone thinks Gilead's Cove was behind it and that your officer was working for the cult."

Alarm flashed through Cassidy when she realized that word had already leaked. How had that happened? She'd tried to keep the news under wraps. "What happened next?"

"I was practically beside myself. I was crying. I mean, Jim and I have a mortgage to pay. We're three months behind, and I'm afraid someone is going to take our house. And that was the final blow. I don't have family to fall back on. I don't have anyone. I can't lose the house, Cassidy."

Cassidy's heart panged with compassion for the woman. Still, she had to press forward with this interview. "I guess that stressed Jim out?"

Rebecca glanced at her hands and drew in a shaky breath. "Yes, you could say that. But I realized that I've been overly emotional lately. Spontaneously, I decided to . . . to take a pregnancy test last night."

Realization rolled over Cassidy. "And?"

Rebecca offered a weak smile. "Jim and I have been trying for eight years. I didn't think I could get pregnant. But I am."

"Congratulations. That's really exciting, Rebecca."

"Thanks." But Rebecca didn't sound happy as her voice dipped. "I want to be excited. But with all our other problems, bringing a baby into the world is scary. I told Jim the news. I thought the announcement might bring him out of his funk. But it made it worse. I've never seen him look so stressed out. He grabbed his keys and left."

As Rebecca said those final words, she crumbled into a ball of tears.

Cassidy moved beside her and put her arm around the woman's shoulders. "He'll come around, Rebecca."

"What if he doesn't?"

"Then you'll be okay because you're a strong woman with a strong community around you. People here aren't going to let you or your new baby down. I know Lantern Beach well enough to know that."

"What am I going to do, Cassidy?" Rebecca

looked up, her eyes orbs of moisture and redness and fear.

"This island is your family. I know it seems bad now, but it will pass. We're not going to let you and your family go homeless or hungry. I can promise you that."

Rebecca sniffled. "You mean that?"

Cassidy nodded. "I do."

"Thank you. Sometimes I think you're the glue that holds this island together, Cassidy."

That was the last thing Cassidy felt like. But she appreciated the encouragement.

CHAPTER TWENTY-THREE

TY SAT UP IN BED, his head pounding. He hadn't felt this ill in a long time.

He was between bouts of sickness, and, despite his headache, for a brief moment, he felt better. At least until the next spell.

He struggled to his feet and lumbered into the kitchen to get some water. As he cleared the hallway, he spotted someone at his front door.

Colton.

Despite his zombie-like state, Ty let him inside.

"You look awful," Colton said, squinting at his friend.

"I think I have food poisoning." Ty pressed his hands against the kitchen counter, his energy already waning after the short walk from his bedroom. "It's wiped me out. You feeling okay?"

"Yeah, I'm fine." Colton continued to squint. "You think it was something you ate yesterday?"

"I wish I knew. I appear to be the only one not feeling well." Ty grabbed a glass, filled it with water, and took a long sip.

"This is probably a bad time, but I wanted to give you an update on something I heard." Colton leaned against the counter. "If you're up for it, of course. I think you'll find my news very interesting."

"Please tell then." Ty drank some more water, hoping his stomach wouldn't cramp up again—for a few minutes, at least.

"I talked to Tom Blackman."

"Who's Tom Blackman?" Ty's head might feel fuzzy right now, but the name didn't even sound vaguely familiar.

"He's the soldier we rescued on that last mission."

Ty's head suddenly cleared. "You were able to find out his name?"

That last mission had been a strange one, where they'd been given only a picture and a location. They knew the man they were rescuing was a captured soldier, but he'd apparently been on a top-secret mission, so the news of a capture—and later his rescue—hadn't been public. Nor had his name.

"Long story, but it turns out Tom and I have some

mutual friends. Anyway, I just got off the phone with him, and he said a few things I thought were very interesting."

"If this ties in with Anthony Gilead in any way, I'm all ears." As Kujo nuzzled him, Ty patted his head.

"I can't say anything for sure concerning a connection with this Gilead guy. You know Tom was beaten pretty badly. He was held captive for three months at the compound."

"And when we rescued him, his back looked exactly like Anthony Gilead's apparently does now." Ty still cringed when he thought about it.

"Exactly. But here's the interesting thing. Tom said he thought there was another American being held there."

Ty's breath caught. "What do you mean?"

"He didn't know anything for sure. But one of the guards had blue eyes—"

"Just like the man you saw," Ty finished, his heart racing with excitement.

"Yes, and Tom thought he heard him trying to speak to him in English once. It was right after a beating, though, so Tom wasn't sure if he was delirious or if it was true."

Ty rubbed a hand over his face, trying to think

this through. "Why would they have an American there? In terrorist garb, at that?"

Colton grabbed one of the dog's water bowls and began filling it as Ranger came over to pant at his feet. "That's what we don't know. This guy freely wandered the compound, but he never had any weapon. It was almost like these guys made him a part of their workforce but didn't fully trust him."

"I don't suppose he had a name?"

Colton shook his head and placed the bowl back on the floor. "No name."

There was still one thing Ty didn't understand . . . "Why didn't this come out earlier?"

"Toward the end, this man started beating Tom as well, so a lot of his doubts about the man's identity vanished. It wasn't until I asked Tom that he really thought it was worth bringing up. It's still all speculation."

"But what if that man was Anthony Gilead?" Was this the missing link they were looking for?

"That's what I'm wondering. I couldn't tell you how he ended up in the Middle East or how he found himself at the mercy of Akrum Abadi. But at least it's a theory, a place to start."

"I'll take a theory over nothing. But now I just need to figure out how to get more information." As

Ty took another sip of water, his stomach churned with nausea.

Colton nodded, his jaw hardening. "That's all Tom remembered. I'd say your best bet would be to track down some people from this guy's past and see what they know."

"I think you're right." Cassidy had already put in some calls about Anthony Gilead from his days as Gerrard Becker. But maybe they could launch that investigation at the next level.

Because this had to end—and soon.

FIELDING CALLED Cassidy and asked her to meet at Dane's place. He had a development he wanted her to see for herself.

He was waiting outside when Cassidy pulled up, and he had a frown on his face.

Whatever this "development" was, it wasn't good.

"Two things I wanted to share with you," Fielding started. "First, we confirmed that Frankie did not have any life insurance policies on his father. Not only that, but Morty Simpson refinanced his house two years ago and actually owes money on it. It's doubtful his son killed him for the money because there apparently wasn't any."

"So is Frankie still a suspect?" Cassidy said.

"Officially, yes. But I agree with your assessment of the man. He doesn't seem bright enough to pull off an operation like this. At least, not without someone's help. And we're not sure we have a motive, though we did talk to his girlfriend, Becky. She said she hasn't noticed anything suspicious."

At least someone had been able to get up with the woman.

"So why are we at Dane's?" Cassidy glanced around, wondering what they'd missed the first time around.

"That's the other thing." Fielding nodded toward the front door. "You'll want to see this for yourself."

Trepidation rose in Cassidy as she climbed the steps. What exactly had they discovered inside? She craved answers, yet she dreaded the results of those potential answers. Her natural inclination was to protect the ones she loved—not lock them away for life.

"We came back here this morning just to do one more sweep of the place, to make sure we didn't miss anything," Fielding explained.

"Okay."

"While we were here, Easton stumbled on the

edge of the rug in the living room." Fielding opened the door and ushered Cassidy inside.

He offered no more explanation. And he didn't need to.

As soon as Cassidy stepped inside, she saw the mark on the floor.

Silently, she walked toward it.

The area rug in front of the couch had been peeled back, revealing a wood floor beneath it. Only, it wasn't just a wood floor.

There, in the center of it, a three-by-three-foot mark had been painted in black. Cassidy had seen it before. It was the Hebrew symbol for M.

The symbol associated with Gilead and the supposed book of the Bible he'd discovered, Makir.

"Why would Dane do this?" Cassidy muttered, unable to take her eyes off it.

"It almost reminds me of something one of those mystical type of cults would do," Fielding said, following her gaze and pressing his lips together in disgust.

"I agree. It reminds me of an antichrist symbol or something. But this doesn't fit with Gilead's Cove. I've never seen anything like this anywhere else. I mean, I've seen the symbol before. Apparently, they brand their members with it. But I've never seen it anywhere besides burned into people's skin."

Fielding flinched. "Yeah, well, who knows what that group is hiding. They don't look like anything but trouble to me. You say the word, and we'll help you find anything we can to shut them down—unpaid taxes, illegal weapons, you name it."

"I won't turn down your help." Cassidy shifted her thoughts for the moment. "Have you talked to Dane yet?"

"No, not yet. He seems more open to talking to you. I thought you might want to take the first crack at him."

"I'd love to," Cassidy said.

Her gaze lingered on the symbol, and a shiver ran up her spine.

She didn't want to believe her officer would do this. But the evidence was becoming irrefutable.

Maybe she should stop looking. Maybe she had the right suspect in custody after all.

CHAPTER TWENTY-FOUR

"DO you really think I would do that, Cassidy?" Dane stared at her through the metal bars of his cell. He looked haggard and worn down, with circles beneath his eyes, the start of a beard, and unkempt hair. The longer he stayed in this cell, the faster he was going downhill.

"It's not a matter of what I think, Dane." Cassidy's jaw tightened as she tried to push aside her emotions. "You know that. It's about following the evidence."

He backed up and crossed his arms, a dark look shadowing his gaze as outrage emanated from him. "I'm being set up."

Cassidy swallowed hard, trying to think this through. She didn't want to be narrow-minded here. If Dane was innocent, he needed someone to fight for him. But if he was guilty, she hoped he went away for life.

"Okay, Dane," she started. "Let's say that's true. If so, who had a key to your house?"

"I'm renting, so the rental company does."

Rebecca's picture fluttered through her mind. It was a possible connection Cassidy needed to keep in mind. "Okay. Who else? Did you give it to any friends?"

Dane raked a hand through his dark hair and began pacing. "I haven't been in town long enough to make many friends. You guys have come over on occasion to let Ranger out for me. I suppose you could have saved the code."

"Noted," Cassidy said. "I'll rule myself out. But that still doesn't tell me how that symbol got there."

"The place used to be a vacation rental. Maybe someone who stayed there before still remembers the code to get in."

"I suppose that's a possibility, but it seems like a long shot, Dane." She had to be truthful with him.

He raked a hand through his hair again, and Cassidy could sense the tension building in him.

"I know it does." Dane dropped back down onto his bed. "But I don't know what else to say. I didn't paint the symbol there. Did it look fresh?"

"It had some wear marks. I'd guess it's been there a month or two."

"Of course. Right about the time I moved here." He frowned.

"Besides, if someone broke in, wouldn't Ranger have alerted you?"

"You would think. But, Cassidy, I don't know how many times I can say this. I didn't do this. Do you believe me?" His gaze locked onto hers.

Cassidy took a step back, knowing she had more work to do. "What I believe doesn't matter. But I don't want this to be you, Dane. I don't."

"Then prove it isn't. Please."

———

AS CASSIDY ENDED her conversation with Dane, she realized something was bugging her. But she couldn't put her finger on what. She needed a moment alone to sort out everything she'd learned today.

"Melva, I need some time in my office uninterrupted," Cassidy said as she emerged from the hallway where the holding cell was located. "Unless it's an emergency, let me work, okay?"

"Of course."

Cassidy shut the door and sat at her desk. She

closed her eyes, trying to make sense of the thoughts waging war in her mind.

What was she missing? What was that thought that begged for her attention? She felt certain it was the one puzzle piece that would allow her to see the bigger picture.

Cassidy hadn't said it aloud, but she didn't believe Dane was behind this. If she trusted her gut, that's what it told her. She didn't see any deceit in her officer's eyes, despite the evidence stacking up against him.

She also didn't think Rebecca was guilty, nor did she really think Frankie was the person responsible— unless he'd worked with someone else.

Cassidy still thought this went back to Anthony Gilead, but he was smart enough not to leave any evidence of that. No, if Gilead was behind this, then he'd gotten someone else to do his dirty work, and he hadn't left any trails.

The thought made anger burn inside.

She was going to nab the man one day. He was going to slip up, and Cassidy was going to be first in line to arrest the man. But, for now, she needed to focus.

Okay, Cassidy, if it's not Dane, Rebecca, or Frankie, then who could it be?

She needed to work under the assumption that

someone had set Dane up. Someone had needed a scapegoat, and Dane had been the chosen one.

He said the management company had the code to his place. There were other renters, but that would have taken a lot of coordination to get a code from one of them. Cassidy didn't think that was what had happened.

She tapped her finger on the desk and closed her eyes.

She'd gone over to Dane's place once or twice to let Ranger out while Dane was working a couple cases. Leggott had done the same. Melva might have even done it a few times.

And so had Abbott . . .

Her thoughts stopped cold.

Abbott?

No . . .

Cassidy flung her eyes open. She didn't like it, but she had to explore this possibility.

What if it was Abbott who'd been leaking information to Gilead's Cove?

The man was definitely smart enough to orchestrate something like this. Yet he hadn't been at Mac's party. Could he be working with someone?

Cassidy really didn't know much about the man, other than what she'd learned working with him a few times in the past. He was from Raleigh. Not married. He seemed to live for his job. Once he'd mentioned that he liked fishing and boating.

The main red flag waving in her mind was the fact that Abbott was in town now, that he wasn't answering his phone, and that he hadn't mentioned anything to Cassidy about being here.

Cassidy was going to have to plan her next steps very carefully. She had no proof right now. She definitely needed something definitive if she was going to pursue this more. She didn't want to throw one of her people under the bus, especially if he wasn't guilty.

But Cassidy felt certain that Abbott was the person she'd been looking for.

Now she needed to find the evidence to solidify her case.

CHAPTER TWENTY-FIVE

CASSIDY ALMOST CALLED Leggott into her office to talk. Then she remembered the microphones and cameras that had been planted there not long ago. She hadn't swept her office recently, and she didn't want to take any chances that Abbott could be listening.

Instead, she asked Leggott to meet her outside under the guise of showing him something in her vehicle.

As they stepped from the office, the sun was starting to set. Soon it would be dark, time to call it quits for the day. Only she couldn't. Wouldn't.

Fielding and Easton were still investigating things at Dane's place. The last update informed Cassidy that the symbol had been left with permanent marker, which was an interesting choice.

If someone had used paint, Dane would have definitely smelled something. But permanent marker . . . the scent would have faded by the time he arrived home.

Was it proof he was innocent? No. But it was something to consider.

"What's going on?" Leggott slid his sunglasses off and put his hands on his hips as he turned to address Cassidy.

Cassidy glanced around before taking a step closer. "Listen, I know we've made an arrest in this case. But I need you to do something for me."

"Anything. What are you thinking?"

"NCSBI Agent Gabe Abbott is on this island somewhere. I need you to figure out where." Cassidy would do it herself, but she needed to try and track down where the man was staying. That required her to be at her desk and on the phone, unfortunately. It wasn't the glamorous side of police work, but it was a definite reality.

Leggott shrugged. "Okay, sure. What do I do when I find out?"

"Just keep an eye on him and report back. I need to know what he's doing here."

Leggott narrowed his eyes. "You think he's involved in this somehow?"

"I don't know anything for sure. That's what I'm trying to figure out."

"Any reason why you called me out here?" He continued to stare as if both curious and suspicious.

"For privacy." As the words left Cassidy's lips, she glanced down at Leggott's hand. A subtle black ink stained the side of his hand—like the kind that might appear after using a permanent marker.

What if that mark hadn't been old after all? Maybe it had been made to look old somehow. Cassidy wasn't sure how viable that reasoning was, but she needed to explore it.

Leggott followed her gaze and rubbed the mark. "What?"

"Where's the ink from?"

"Just from writing up some reports. I use black ink, and it must not have dried. What's the big deal?"

Cassidy pressed her lips together. She wouldn't tip him off. Not yet.

First, she needed to see how all of this would play out.

MELVA LEFT THIRTY MINUTES LATER, leaving Cassidy alone at the station—other than Dane.

She called Ty, who said he was feeling a little

better. But she could tell he was not in the right frame of mind to help her.

Instead, she called Mac. He promised to meet her at the station, where Cassidy would update him on today's developments.

While Leggott tried to track down Abbott on foot, Cassidy slipped into the lobby—an area likely not bugged—to make some calls, trying to pinpoint where he was staying on the island. Several phone calls later, she still had no answers.

As a last resort, she called Rebecca Jarvis to see if she could help.

"I don't work for the rental side of the company," she said, her voice still sounding high-pitched and emotional.

"I know. But you have connections, and that's what I need right now."

Rebecca said nothing for a moment. "I'll see what I can find out. Especially if this clears me. I could use some good news."

"No word from Jim?" Cassidy asked.

"Not yet."

"I'll keep praying."

"Thanks, Cassidy. I need all the prayers I can get."

Cassidy ended the call and leaned back in her chair, biding her time until she heard back. Thankfully, Rebecca called back five minutes later.

"Okay, this is what I got," Rebecca said. "You didn't hear it from me. Privacy laws and all. I have enough trouble already."

"Got it. I'll keep you out of this, Rebecca."

She rattled off an address linked with Abbott, as well as the keycode.

Just as Cassidy stood, ready to investigate more, Mac walked into the station. She nodded toward the door.

"We need to go somewhere," Cassidy said.

"You look like a woman on a mission." Mac fell into step beside her.

"I am." For the first time, Cassidy actually felt like she was close to getting some answers. She hoped she was right. She would have to leave Dane alone here at the station for a little while. She had no other choice.

She headed down the road toward the rental house where Abbott was staying, filling Mac in as she drove.

"But you said Leggott had ink on his hands," Mac said.

Cassidy nibbled the inside of her lips before nodding. "That's correct."

"Was the mark on Dane's floor left recently?"

"It's hard to say whether or not it's fresh. There were what appeared to be wear marks. I suppose someone could have sanded it down to make it look that way."

"So you think someone got into Dane's place and left the symbol on the floor in order to frame him?"

"This is all speculation at this point," Cassidy said.

"If Leggott did this, then why are we tracking down Abbott?"

"Because he's in town. And he ate at The Docks yesterday. I've always felt like the man had ulterior motives, and now he's back on the island for no apparent reason. He had the code to get into Dane's place, and the man is smart."

"It does seem suspicious, though it doesn't necessarily mean he's guilty."

Dark lined the windows as they traveled down the road, darkness that could be a friend or a foe. Right now, Cassidy hoped it would offer them the cover they needed. "I know that. I really do. But I have to follow every lead."

"You don't think Dane did this, do you?" Mac glanced at her.

Cassidy shook her head. "No, I don't."

"Then let's go check out Abbott's place."

Cassidy tried to call Leggott to see if he'd located Abbott yet, but her officer's phone went to voicemail. Cassidy ended the call and frowned.

"What is it?" Mac asked.

"Leggott isn't answering."

"Maybe he's in the middle of something."

"Maybe he is, but it's not like him." Cassidy pulled to a stop three houses down from Abbott's rental. There were no cars in the driveway at his place, and, if he came back, Cassidy didn't want to alert him that she was here.

She glanced over at Mac, gearing herself up for action. "Let's do this. But we have to be discreet."

"I'm in."

CHAPTER TWENTY-SIX

CASSIDY CAREFULLY TYPED in the numerical code to Abbott's rental and slipped inside, Mac behind her.

Standing just inside the front door, Cassidy scanned the great room. From her vantage point, she saw nothing and no one. This part of the house was empty and practically appeared untouched.

"What are you expecting to find here?" Mac whispered.

"I have no idea," Cassidy admitted. "Would it be too broad to say answers?"

"Probably."

"I guess I'll know it when I see it then."

Mac headed to the left, into the living room, while Cassidy went right toward the kitchen. She scanned everything as she walked, not touching anything—

yet. First, she needed to scope out the house for trouble and make sure it was clear.

She paused by the dining room table.

Papers were scattered across the glass top, the only visible evidence anyone had been here. Cassidy glanced down and saw letters addressed to the county manager concerning some property here on the island.

Melva. Melva had signed these letters.

Realization washed over her.

"Mac, we need to get to Melva's place."

Mac strode across the room and stood beside her. "What's up?"

"I think Abbott is going after her." She held up the papers.

Alarm spread through his gaze. "Okay. Let's not waste any more time."

Melva lived only two streets over. As they rushed toward her house, she handed Mac the papers. "Can you make anything out about these?"

He scanned the words there. "Just that Melva was unhappy about her house being taken away. You think Abbott decided to capitalize on that?"

"I think there's a good chance of that. Find a weakness and exploit it. Isn't that what evil people do?"

Before they could chat more, they pulled up to

Melva's place. All the lights were off, and two cars were in the driveway—Melva's and Abbott's.

When they reached the front door, Cassidy twisted the knob. It was unlocked.

She exchanged a look with Mac before stepping inside, her gun drawn. "Police!"

She flipped on the lights but saw no one. Had Abbott come here, found Melva, and taken her somewhere?

Cautiously, they began a search of the perimeter.

Cassidy had only made it a few steps when movement sounded in the distance.

Mac's eyes met hers across the room.

Was someone here?

On alert, Cassidy moved toward the noise. It almost sounded like it came from the pantry, which was located at the edge of the kitchen, near the hallway.

Still gripping her gun, she carefully approached the door. Bracing herself, she counted to three and jerked it open.

Her eyes widened when she saw Abbott inside the spacious closet, tied to a chair, with a gag stuffed into his mouth.

Cassidy reached forward, about to pull the cloth from his mouth.

Before she could, something clicked behind them.

Cassidy and Mac turned to see Leggott standing there, panic across his expression.

Melva held him with one arm. Her other hand gripped a gun, its tip pressing into Leggott's temple.

Melva?

What was going on here?

———

"PUT your guns down or I'll shoot him," Melva barked. "I mean it."

As if to drive home the point, Leggott flinched with pain. That's when Cassidy noticed the blood trickling down his forehead.

What had happened before they arrived? Melva must have been hiding in one of the bedrooms. Had she been anticipating they'd come?

"No need to panic, Melva." Cassidy lowered her gun to the floor. "We'll cooperate."

Mac placed his gun on the floor also and backed up a step.

"I didn't want it to come to this," Melva said, her lips pulled into a tight line as she paused. "You caught on to things more quickly than I thought you would."

"You framed Dane for this crime." Cassidy kept

an eye on Melva's gun as she tried to formulate a plan that wouldn't get them all killed.

"Of course I did. I couldn't take the fall."

"Why would you do any of this, Melva?" Mac asked. "It isn't like you."

"Isn't like me? How would any of you know? None of you know what I'm like." Her words contained a bitter edge.

Cassidy watched as Leggott squirmed. The gun remained jammed into his temple, and his body was bent at an awkward angle to accommodate Melva's short height. Sweat covered his forehead and neck.

"Let's talk this through, Melva," Cassidy said. "There's no need for anyone to get hurt."

"I'm already going to jail. I'm in serious trouble. You said so yourself last night when you talked about the person responsible for this. I don't have anything to lose."

"There's always something to lose," Mac said. "You have a daughter and granddaughter."

Melva sneered. "They never even speak with me anymore. Never make an effort to visit. I make no difference to them. I'm expendable. Every part of me. Everything I own."

It must be horrible to live feeling so worthless. But Melva's words weren't true.

"You might be surprised, Melva," Cassidy said.

"We're like a family at the police department. You're one of us. You do make a difference."

Melva's gaze softened but only for a moment before reigniting with an even stronger burst of anger. "Enough talking! I've got to figure out what to do with all of you."

Cold fear crept down Cassidy's spine. Melva had lost it. Gone was the sweet, awkward woman who answered the phone at the station. This crazy woman had taken her place.

"What are you thinking?" Cassidy asked, trying to get into the woman's head.

"I don't know." Melva's voice rose to a level Cassidy didn't think possible. "It wasn't supposed to come to this."

"How did you see this playing out, Melva?" Mac asked, remaining calm and in control beside Cassidy. His years of experience were showing, and Cassidy hoped her outside expression matched his. "How did you think it would end?"

"With Dane going to jail, of course. I set up all the evidence. Made sure he was at the party."

"His fingerprints were on the piping bag," Cassidy said, wondering how she'd managed that.

Melva smiled and jammed the gun into Leggott's head again, making him whimper. "That's right. Remember those Easter bunnies I made not long ago? They were out of these bags. I twisted them so you couldn't even tell and then gave one to each of you, making sure you all touched them. Then I collected them after the holiday so I could use them again at my discretion. No one noticed, and *voila!* I got a fingerprint. You guys aren't the only ones who are clever. I've got it in me sometimes."

"And you drew that symbol under his rug?" Cassidy hoped that with time she could talk some sense into Melva. She just needed to get her warmed up first. At this point, it was the only solution Cassidy could think of that would keep them all safe.

"I did. I knew you'd want something more solid. That's the nice part about working at the station. I get to see how you operate and think. I get to listen to your phone calls. Sometimes, I've even seen your emails. It's been a good learning experience."

"And, after Dane was framed, you planned to continue working at the police station . . ." Cassidy finished. "Gathering intel and using it to your advantage."

The thought of it turned Cassidy's stomach. Was there any such thing as loyalty anymore? Cassidy was beginning to doubt it.

"That was the plan. But I could tell you didn't really think Officer Bradshaw was guilty. I knew you weren't going to drop this." She shoved the gun again, and Leggott sucked in a sharp gasp.

Adrenaline pulsed through Cassidy. This situation could turn ugly fast, and she needed to speed up this process of talking Melva down from the ledge. It wasn't working yet. The woman's voice seemed to get louder and her motions more frantic by the moment.

"Just tell me this, Melva," Cassidy said. "Why? Why would you do all of this?"

Her neck twitched as if she was about to share a conviction so strong it had consumed her thoughts and taken over her central nervous system. "Because Anthony Gilead will make a great mayor on this island. He actually cares about the people."

"You don't think I care about the people of this island, Melva?" Mac's voice sounded wounded—though Cassidy was sure that was on purpose.

Melva's shoulders drooped, but just for a moment. Then it was like she remembered all her bitterness and tensed even more. She was obviously battling within herself. Who knew how long this had been building? She was past the point of no return now.

"No one on this island sees me," she snapped. "No one saw me but Anthony Gilead."

"How did you meet him?" Cassidy was still trying to buy time.

The only people who could help her right now were indisposed. Ty was sick. Dane was locked up. She had no idea where Fielding and Easton were, but she hadn't told them she was coming here.

Cassidy's eyes hardly left that gun pressed into Leggott's head, though. One wrong move and . . . she couldn't even think about it.

"I take a walk every morning before work. I ran into him there."

Cassidy would guess that was no coincidence, that Gilead had followed Melva's schedule and arranged to "run into her." "What happened then?"

Melva's face softened. "He was so wonderful. It was like he could see inside my life and he knew just how broken I was. Not only that, he knew how to fix me."

That seemed to be a common theme with people who were a part of the cult. Most came from poor, hard backgrounds. Most were at the end of their ropes or had substance abuse problems. Gilead offered them another chance, the opportunity to make things better.

"So you joined the Cause?" Cassidy clarified.

"Not really. Gilead gave me some books. We

would meet on our walks sometimes, and he'd talk to me."

"But he asked you to be a spy?" Bile rose in Cassidy's stomach at the thought.

"No, he never asked me to be a spy. But I wanted to help him. I told him that he and his followers were under police scrutiny."

"And he said?"

"That the information was helpful. He thanked me for sharing. After that, it just seemed natural to keep him in the loop. He did so much for me that I wanted to help him. He can bring so much good to this world. It's what we should all want. We need more Anthony Gileads."

"Did he ask you to rig the election?" Mac asked.

Melva let out a short, bitter laugh. "No, of course not. Gilead would never do anything like that. I had to think of a way to get him in office, though. If he could revitalize my life, just think of what he could do for everyone here on the island." Melva's voice continued to climb, and her pupils looked dilated. The woman was on the verge of doing something really, really stupid.

"He's a dangerous man, Melva," Cassidy said. Gilead was even more dangerous because no one could see just how dangerous he was.

"No, he's gentle. Kind. He cares about me and everyone under him." Her arms jerked at the notion.

Cassidy held her breath, waiting for disaster to happen.

"He's got you fooled," Mac said. "There are other people who can help you. People who don't want your money or don't care about what you can do for them. Just good, honest people. Sometimes people just need a little nudge before they step in to help."

"Stop talking!" Melva fired the gun.

Everyone froze.

Cassidy held her breath, waiting to see if Leggott would crumple to the ground. He remained standing.

Her gaze traveled upward, and she spotted the hole in the ceiling. Melva had shot the gun through the roof.

Cassidy's heart pounded even harder in her ears. Melva was losing it. Maybe she'd been losing it for a while.

What Cassidy had assumed to be social anxiety had probably been stress as Melva gathered information for Gilead.

But Melva fit the profile of someone Gilead would target. She was lonely. Hurting. Had little to live for.

In fact, the woman was the perfect ghost. She was

someone who hardly ever got noticed. Someone who stayed under the radar.

Melva had let Ranger out at least once. Cassidy clearly remembered it. When Cassidy hadn't been able to go herself, Melva had volunteered.

Yet last night Melva had definitely acted uncomfortable around dogs.

The day she had let Ranger out, she had claimed she didn't mind them. Was it because volunteering to help with the dog had given Melva the perfect excuse to get into Dane's place? Had she left the symbol there under the rug, setting this all up?

Melva would have known the dates of the election, known she would need to act on the food poisoning the day before the polling site opened.

And she claimed to not know much about salmonella but . . .

Cassidy reviewed everything she could remember from the woman's file. Where had her deceased husband worked? Huntington Rawlings. What kind of company was that?

A light went on in Cassidy's mind. She vaguely recalled Lisa talking to Melva about it once. Melva had mentioned something about her husband testing blood samples in some kind of lab. That's what Huntington Rawlings was!

And Melva fit the profile of someone who would

join Gilead's Cove. She was lonely. She had no one. She'd seemingly lost her sense of purpose.

How could Cassidy have not seen this?

Another thought hit her, causing her to draw in a quick breath. What if Melva had made Ty sick last night?

The woman had gone to get a refill on her coffee and had offered to take Ty's cup. What if she'd contaminated it when she did so? It was the only thing that made sense. Melva had wanted to make sure Ty was out of commission.

She'd even offered to get Cassidy some coffee, but Cassidy had refused, knowing the caffeine would keep her up too late.

Melva sneered, her nostrils flaring and pupils dilating even more. Cassidy could see the emotion and bitterness rising in her and braced herself for whatever was about to happen.

"I see only one way to end this," Melva said. "By killing you all."

Then she raised her gun toward Cassidy.

CHAPTER TWENTY-SEVEN

AS ANOTHER GUNSHOT rang out across the room, Cassidy waited to feel a bullet hit her chest. Waited to feel pain. For her world to go black.

Instead, Melva sank to the floor.

Mac darted forward and grabbed her gun as the woman bled. He grabbed a dish towel from the counter and pressed it into her wound to stop the bleeding.

Cassidy's gaze traveled across the room. Fielding and Easton stood at the door. Fielding held a gun, and his expression was grim.

Her shoulders sagged in relief.

She was okay. So were Leggott, Mac, and Abbott.

Fielding was already on the phone calling the rescue squad as Melva grasped her chest and moaned with pain. Cassidy stepped toward her but paused and glanced at her officer.

"You okay, Leggott?" Cassidy called.

He rubbed his neck, his body bent over with distress. But he nodded before lowering himself onto the couch and staring off in the distance. No doubt he was feeling some shock right now.

She'd give him a minute before talking to him more. Instead, she knelt beside Melva. "You didn't have to do this, you know."

Melva's eyes squeezed shut. "I . . . don't . . . regret . . . anything."

"How much did you tell Gilead?" Cassidy continued.

Melva said nothing.

"How much did you tell him?" Cassidy repeated.

Melva's eyes snapped open, her pain-filled gaze meeting Cassidy's. "I told him anything I thought would help him. He's not your enemy, Cassidy. He only wants what's best for this island."

With those last words, Melva closed her eyes again.

EMTs rushed into the room—they must have been close—and took over. As they did, Cassidy stepped back and lifted up a prayer for the woman. She had to be absolutely desperate to have done what she did

. . .

Instead of feeling satisfied that the case had been concluded, all Cassidy felt was disturbed.

———

AS FIELDING and Easton took over the scene, Cassidy wandered to Abbott.

"Are you hurt?" she asked him.

He shook his head, but grimaced as he shook out his arms and legs, as if his body was stiff. "I'm fine."

"How did you get pulled into this?" Cassidy had nearly forgotten the man was here. He'd been forcibly quiet behind them, and his presence was forgotten as they'd faced Melva and her gun.

"I was thinking about everything happening here," Abbott said. "And I started looking into everyone's background in the police department."

Cassidy felt the blood drain from her face. "Why would you do that?"

Something unreadable glimmered in his eyes. "Because I have a feeling one of you has been tipping off Anthony Gilead about what's going on in our investigations."

"Why would you say that?" Cassidy knew exactly why he'd say that, but she needed to hear it with her own ears.

"There's no way Anthony Gilead should get off

scot-free of these crimes. We all know he's connected to them. But he somehow knows what's going to happen in advance. He and his people can destroy the evidence and claim innocence. I don't buy it."

"So you think me or one of my people is behind it?" Cassidy clarified.

"That's right. You're the only ones who make sense."

"And when did you begin this investigation, exactly?" Cassidy thought about those texts she'd received from someone claiming to know about her past. Could it have been Abbott?

"A couple weeks ago. I decided to look into Melva and saw she'd written stacks of letters complaining to the state about how her home near the ferry docks had been taken. It's been going on for years. She sends one every month or so."

"She mentioned the county took away her home," Cassidy said.

"From reading the letters, I gathered this was the home she'd lived in with her husband," Abbott said. "I started thinking I could use that information to gain her trust and find out more information on everyone in the department. Well, not everyone. After all, Leggott and Bradshaw were squeaky clean."

Cassidy noticed he didn't include her but said nothing about it.

"I came here to talk to her," Abbott continued. "But when I stopped by, Melva went crazy. She must have thought I knew something I didn't. She pulled a gun, forced me into this closet, and knocked me out. Next thing I knew, I woke up and saw you all."

"That's unfortunate," Cassidy said. "I guess I was wrong about you, Abbott."

"Wait, you thought *I* was acting as an informant to the cult?" He cocked an eyebrow up, arrogance returning to his features.

Cassidy shrugged. "I did wonder about it."

"I'm not that kind of guy. If anything, I'm a bit of a pessimist. Ask my ex-wife."

"I'll take your word for it." The sooner Abbott was out of her life, the better.

He stepped closer and narrowed his eyes at Cassidy. "And your background was surprisingly lacking."

An underlying threat tinged his words.

Cassidy held her head high. "Is that right?"

"Is there anything you need to tell me, Chief?"

"Absolutely not."

"Are you sure?"

Before Cassidy could respond, Fielding stepped up beside them. "Everyone okay?"

"I think so," Cassidy said, composing herself. "You showed up just in time. How did you know?"

"We put in a call to the company that sells those salmonella samples. We asked if anyone in this area had ordered any. Melva's husband's name came up. She must have used his identity when placing the order. We tried to call you, but you didn't answer."

"I didn't even hear it ring." Cassidy pulled her phone out. She looked through her contacts and squinted. "It looks like your number has been blocked on my phone."

"I guess you might attribute that to Melva," Fielding said. "Did she have access to it?"

Cassidy nodded. "I'm sure she did at times."

"The good news is that I think this is all over. She pretty much confessed to everything, and we all heard it. If she survives this, she'll be in prison for a long time."

"At least justice has been served," Cassidy said.

"Yes, we all have some answers now."

Cassidy stepped toward Leggott. He appeared visibly shaken by what had happened. He sat on the couch still trying to catch his breath. "You doing okay?"

She knew he was physically okay, but emotionally might be another story.

He shrugged, his eyes bloodshot and his motions

shaky. "I really don't know. I thought I saw Abbott in his car—someone told me they'd seen him at The Docks and he'd mentioned staying near Anchor Lane. I saw him driving by, followed him, and then I realized he was headed to Melva's place."

"What happened next?"

"I parked at the end of the road and tried to call you. You didn't answer. So I decided to check things out myself. When I got to the door, Melva looked crazy. She had a gun in her hand and forced me inside. Next thing I knew, we were hiding out in the back because she heard you guys pull up."

"I'm sorry, Leggott."

He looked up at her, regret in his gaze. "I think it's time, Chief."

"Time for what?" Cassidy tilted her head in confusion.

"It's time for me to move on from Lantern Beach. It's been a good run, and I've learned a lot from you. But I'm ready to start new. This seals the deal, if you know what I mean."

She nodded slowly. "I understand. You have to do what's best for you. I'll always appreciate your time here."

"Thanks, Chief. And I can leave now knowing this is over. Most of it, at least."

There was still a large chunk that needed to be

figured out, starting with how to rescue everyone involved with Anthony Gilead.

As much as Cassidy wanted to believe this was over, she still had a long road ahead of her.

CHAPTER TWENTY-EIGHT

MORIAH BLINKED as brightness shone in the distance.

Light.

Light had crept into the old bunker. Someone must have opened the door to the outside.

Her excitement quickly turned to fear.

Was it Gilead? What would he do now?

And how long had she even been down here? She couldn't keep track of time in the darkness.

All she'd been able to do was count her tears. Count her mistakes and failures.

When she came to Lantern Beach she thought she'd turned her life around. Instead, she'd fallen into the same old traps. Insecurity had earned her a new batch of heartache, this one worse than the last.

Her arm ached so badly. She hadn't been able to

sit down all night. No, she'd simply sagged against the wall as exhaustion claimed her. Her legs felt weak. Her head swam.

As the minutes had ticked by, her terror had finally subsided, but only a little.

The "what if" questions had haunted her, the biggest one being: What if Gilead left her down here to die? Because this would be a horrible way to spend her final moments.

What else had her husband done down here? What acts of torture or pain?

She could hardly think about it.

Moriah blinked again and stared at the light, trying to see who was coming down the steps. But her eyes burned at the brightness until moisture streamed down her face.

She was surprised she had any tears left.

After all, she was so thirsty. And hungry.

She may have even passed out a few times last night. She couldn't be sure. In some ways, everything was a blur. In other ways, every detail felt sharp and unforgettable.

She blinked again as a figure came into view.

It wasn't Gilead.

It was a woman.

Ruth?

"Moriah, we've got to get you out of here," someone whispered.

Moriah fluttered her eyelashes, desperate to clear her vision. Was that . . . "Serena?"

"This was the first chance I had to get away without being seen." Serena began working the shackle at Moriah's wrist. She had some kind of bobby pin in her hand. "I followed you this morning, but Gilead has people watching everything."

"You're helping me?"

"He's going to kill you eventually, Moriah. You know that, right?"

The reminder solidified the ball of dread in her stomach. Serena was right. "Gilead will kill us both if he finds you down here."

"That's why we have to move and move quickly."

The shackle released, and Moriah's arm fell to her side. Relief instantly eased through her muscles. She rubbed the skin where the metal had been and felt the raw flesh there.

Serena grabbed her good hand, urgency filling her voice and actions. "Come on. Let's go."

Moriah took a step forward but crumpled on the ground. No food. No water. No sleep.

Her body was already so weak. It didn't want to cooperate.

"We can do this," Serena whispered. "You can rest later."

Moriah nodded, knowing what Serena said was true. She tried to stand, only to fall again.

Serena went to her side, slipped an arm around her waist, and helped her up.

But as they took a step toward the door, a shadow filled it.

Moriah let out a desperate cry.

Now that her sight had adjusted to the light, she could clearly see a man there.

More panic surged through her, and she gripped Serena's arm.

Moriah and Serena both were going to be trapped here, and she could only imagine what the punishment for their disobedience would be.

CHAPTER TWENTY-NINE

CASSIDY GLANCED around The Crazy Chefette at her friends. Lisa and Braden were there, along with Austin and Skye, Wes, Mac, and Jack and Juliette. Colton had also shown up, as had Carter Denver.

Ty had come, but he still wasn't 100 percent yet. At least he'd stopped throwing up. They'd talked just a little last night, and he'd told her about his conversation with Colton—about the lead he had on Anthony Gilead's missing years.

But, right now, for a moment—and just a moment—it felt like old times. It felt like things weren't falling apart. That there was hope for this island.

Lisa had been cleared to open this weekend, after all.

Fielding and Easton had taken Melva into

custody. She was in ICU at a hospital in Raleigh, but doctors expected her to recover.

Meanwhile, Dane had been released. Cassidy had spoken with him last night, and he seemed both relieved to be free and disappointed to hear about Melva. Either way, he didn't appear to be holding a grudge against Cassidy or the department. She was thankful for that. She couldn't lose another officer.

The good news was that Braden was going to step up and take Leggott's place. He'd been cleared for the workforce, and Cassidy thought he'd make a great addition to their team.

"Well, it looks like you did it again, Chief." Mac stepped up beside her and watched the crowd also. They stood on the edge of the room where they had a clear view of everyone and even the doors.

Sometimes, it was hard to stop being a cop. It was in her blood to keep an eye on things, whether she liked it or not.

"I did, even though I feel like it was by the skin of my teeth," Cassidy finally said.

"I still can't believe Melva was behind this," Mac said. "I didn't know the woman well, but she seemed more like the type to bake cookies for her coworkers rather than poison salad dressing and kill someone."

"I can't either. Of all the people who were on my radar, she was never one of them."

That had made her the perfect person for the task. It also reminded Cassidy to always keep her eyes open for those who were feeling lonely. Some people let it be known when they were hurting, but others stuffed it inside and tried to disappear.

"If it makes you feel better, she wasn't on anyone's radar."

"Not really." Cassidy bit back a frown. "Especially when considering that Melva was privy to all the information she needed and could report back to Gilead."

A knock sounded on the door behind them. Cassidy looked back and saw Niles Shepherd standing at the entrance to The Crazy Chefette. She unlocked the door and let him inside.

Everyone seemed to notice his arrival and quieted.

He cleared his throat before turning toward Mac. "I just thought you should know that I've heard an official word from the County Board of Elections. They've ruled that the results of our recent mayoral race were invalid, and we're scheduled for a new election in two weeks."

A cheer rose in the air.

"So Anthony Gilead won't be our mayor?" Cassidy asked, confirming she'd heard correctly.

Niles shrugged. "That depends on what happens

in two weeks. But I recommend no one have any parties the night before."

Cassidy almost wanted to laugh, but she couldn't.

"That's great news," Mac said. "Thanks for letting us know, Niles. Why don't you stay for a bite to eat?"

Niles scanned the crowd and shrugged. "I couldn't intrude."

"You wouldn't be. Come on in," Cassidy said. "There's always room for one more here."

To her surprise, Niles shrugged again and took a step forward. "I suppose I could stay for a moment. At least it gets me away from all those awful people at my office who continue to make cat jokes at my expense. I think I'm going to start the Meow Too movement. And don't think I'm joking."

Lisa welcomed him, handed him a plate, and then moseyed over to Cassidy as Mac left to chat with Colton.

"You seem perkier," Cassidy said. "Feeling better?"

All the light hadn't quite returned to Lisa's eyes, but she nodded, not appearing as burdened either. "I'm hoping you're right and that tourists will be able to look past this incident. Honestly, it's all out of my hands at this point. I've spent a lot of time talking to God about accepting the things in my life that I can't change. It's a hard lesson, but it is possible."

"Yes, it is."

"I do have one surprise."

"What's that?"

Lisa reached into the hostess stand and pulled out a . . . book. She handed it to Cassidy.

"I've been secretly working on this project," Lisa said. "I want you to have the first copy."

Cassidy glanced down at the glossy book titled *Cooking with the Crazy Chefette*. "A recipe book? That's a wonderful idea, Lisa."

"I'll just sell them here in the store and online. It's been a nice distraction to work on it, especially with everything that's been going on."

"I think this is great. I'm so honored you gave me this first copy."

"Well, without your hard work, people may have always thought I was behind that food poisoning incident. So thank you." She shifted. "Now we just need to get Serena out of Gilead's Cove and get Mac elected as mayor."

Her words brought Cassidy back to reality.

"As you just heard, we're going to have a new election in two weeks," Cassidy said. "Serena is another story."

"I wish that girl would return to her senses," Lisa said.

"Everyone does."

"Has anything happened to show signs that she might leave on her own?"

Cassidy shook her head, wishing she had better news. Ty joined them, slipping an arm around her waist and still looking paler than Cassidy would like. She probably needed to get him home, but she'd at least wanted to stop by for a bit.

"No, Serena is headstrong," Cassidy continued. "You know how she likes to try on different personalities? Well, this just might be the longest she's ever tried to be someone else."

"I hope she's okay," Lisa said.

"We all do," Ty added.

"But enough about that for now," Cassidy said. "Let's celebrate your book and your restaurant opening again. It will be nice to have a little distraction in the midst of all the craziness lately."

"I agree. Let's eat!"

Cassidy took a step toward the food. But, as she did, she knew she was only pretending to be distracted. She couldn't forget about the trouble on this island. Because the final showdown hadn't happened yet—but she could feel it was getting closer.

COMING IN MAY: PLAN OF ACTION

LANTERN BEACH P.D., BOOK 5

Police Chief Cassidy Chambers took a bite of her grilled cheese and peach sandwich, savoring the unusual flavor combination. She had to get back to work, but she wanted to enjoy the time with her friends for a little longer—and grab a little food.

She and her friends had gathered for an early lunch after an especially stressful couple of days on Lantern Beach. The good news was that her friend Lisa had finally been cleared of her supposed role in a food poisoning epidemic, and the local mayoral election had been rescheduled and the old results tossed out.

They had those two things to celebrate, at least. For a moment, Cassidy wouldn't think about all the worries that still wanted to creep into her mind like guests who'd outstayed their welcome.

Cassidy took the last bite of her sandwich, tossed her plate in the trash, and moseyed over to her husband, Ty. He sat at the table with their friends, but his mind looked like it was a million miles away as he rested his head on a hand splayed across his forehead.

Ty wasn't acting like himself at all right now. It could be the effects of the food poisoning, but Ty looked like he needed to lie down and get away from the world for a while.

Cassidy laid her hand on his arm and leaned closer. "You look like you should go home."

He didn't argue—a sure sign he wasn't feeling well. Instead, he stood and walked with her to the edge of the room, away from an especially rowdy conversation about who was the best volleyball player in the group.

"I hate to admit it, but I think maybe you're right."

"You hate to admit I'm right?" Cassidy teased.

"I hate to admit you're right about needing to leave." He looked like he tried to smile, like he wanted to banter, but he couldn't. Instead, he flinched, and his hand went to his stomach.

Maybe she shouldn't be teasing him right now.

"I know, baby. I'm sorry you're not feeling well."

Cassidy reached for the keys in her pocket. "I can drive you."

Ty waved her off, but his face still looked pale and clammy. "No, I'll be fine. You get your work done at the office. I know you have a ton of paperwork. Then come home early. Maybe I'll feel better by then."

She squinted with concern. She'd be there for him in a heartbeat if he needed her. But it would be nice to knock out some paperwork, if possible. "Are you sure? I don't mind taking you home and staying with you. I could even bring some of my files back to the house and—"

"I'll be fine, Cassidy." He lowered his hand from his abdomen and nodded, not quite selling his words. "I'd rather you not see me like this. I think if I get some rest, I'll be good to go."

"If you're sure." She knew sometimes the former Navy SEAL needed to maintain a little of his macho tendencies and didn't want to push or baby him.

"I am." Ty leaned forward and kissed her cheek. "Good job on solving that last case, by the way. Everyone here on the island owes you their thanks."

"I'm just doing my job."

"We all know it's more than a job to you." He stepped back and offered a slight wave, followed by a wink. "I'll call you later."

"Sounds good, hon. Love you."

Ty smiled. "Love you too, Cassidy."

Cassidy watched as he walked away, feeling a burst of love inside her. Ty was the man of her dreams, and, though it had been a hard road to find each other, she wouldn't change a thing.

She hated the fact he still felt ill. At least the person responsible for making everyone on the island sick was now in custody. With the election rescheduled, maybe the island could finally get back on track. The past few days had been rough on everyone.

But when Ty was by her side, she felt like she could conquer the world. Cassidy knew the island still had a lot of struggles—and they would until Anthony Gilead could be revealed for who he really was. But she couldn't wait until Ty was back to himself so they could face these problems together.

———

Ty's head swam as he headed down the road in his vintage Chevy truck.

He hadn't let on to Cassidy just how bad he was feeling. His head hurt. Nausea roiled in his stomach. All he wanted to do was lie down.

Thankfully, The Crazy Chefette wasn't far from their house. He couldn't get there soon enough.

His hands gripped the steering wheel as he stared at the beautiful day ahead. It was just past lunchtime, and the past few days had passed like a blur. The good news was that Anthony Gilead hadn't really won the election. Not yet, at least.

Knowing Gilead, he probably had something else up his sleeve. The man was power hungry.

Ty's stomach tightened even more.

He hadn't been able to stop thinking about what his friend Colton had told him. Apparently, during their last mission, as they'd rescued their target, there may have been another American there. Had he been working for Akrum Abadi? Or had he been a captive forced into slavery at the compound?

And what was this man's tie with Anthony Gilead? Could the man *be* Anthony Gilead?

The questions continued to squeeze Ty.

One thing he knew for sure: Anthony Gilead hadn't come to this island by mistake. His presence here was no coincidence. And he was somehow connected with Ty.

What he didn't know was the man's end game. What he wanted. Why he was targeting Ty and Cassidy.

Just then, his phone rang. When he saw it was his friend Colton, he answered and put it on speaker. "Hey, man. What's up?"

"I just heard something I thought you might find interesting."

"What's that?" Ty glanced behind him and saw a truck in his rear-view mirror coming up on him fast. He maintained his speed and waited for the vehicle to pass.

Three seconds later, the man was on his tail, nearly running him off the road.

"What's your hurry?" Ty muttered.

"What was that?" Colton said.

"Nothing." Ty glanced in the mirror again and saw the truck remained close—too close. Hopefully, the guy would pass instead of acting like a jerk. "Sorry about that. Go ahead. What did you hear?"

"It's about Anthony Gilead."

Ty's pulse spiked at the mention of the man's name. "I'm all ears."

Before he could listen to what Colton had to say, the engine of the truck behind him revved. The driver jerked into the other lane to go around Ty.

Just as the truck with its dark-tinted windows pulled beside him, it veered into Ty's lane.

The vehicle collided with Ty's, hitting hard.

His truck swerved, but it was no use.

He careened toward the massive ditch at the side of the road.

As his body rammed into the steering wheel, everything went black.

ALSO BY CHRISTY BARRITT:

LANTERN BEACH MYSTERIES

Hidden Currents

You can take the detective out of the investigation, but you can't take the investigator out of the detective. A notorious gang puts a bounty on Detective Cady Matthews's head after she takes down their leader, leaving her no choice but to hide until she can testify at trial. But her temporary home across the country on a remote North Carolina island isn't as peaceful as she initially thinks. Living under the new identity of Cassidy Livingston, she struggles to keep her investigative skills tucked away, especially after a body washes ashore. When local police bungle the murder investigation, she can't resist stepping in. But Cassidy is supposed to be keeping a low profile. One wrong move could lead to both her discovery and her demise. Can she bring justice to the island . . . or will the hidden currents surrounding her pull her under for good?

Flood Watch

The tide is high, and so is the danger on Lantern Beach. Still in hiding after infiltrating a dangerous gang, Cassidy Livingston just has to make it a few more months before she can testify at trial and resume her old life. But trouble keeps finding her, and Cassidy is pulled into a local investigation after a man mysteriously disappears from the island she now calls home. A recurring nightmare from her time undercover only muddies things, as does a visit from the parents of her handsome ex-Navy SEAL neighbor. When a friend's life is threatened, Cassidy must make choices that put her on the verge of blowing her cover. With a flood watch on her emotions and her life in a tangle, will Cassidy find the truth? Or will her past finally drown her?

Storm Surge

A storm is brewing hundreds of miles away, but its effects are devastating even from afar. Laid-back, loose, and light: that's Cassidy Livingston's new motto. But when a makeshift boat with a bloody cloth inside washes ashore near her oceanfront home, her detective instincts shift into gear . . . again. Seeking clues isn't the only thing on her mind—romance is heating up with next-door neighbor and former Navy SEAL Ty Chambers as well. Her heart wants the love and stability she's longed for her entire life. But her hidden identity only leads to a tidal wave of turbulence. As more answers emerge about the boat, the danger around her rises, creating a treacherous swell that threatens to reveal her past. Can Cassidy mind her own business, or will the storm surge of violence and corruption that has washed ashore on Lantern Beach leave her life in wreckage?

Dangerous Waters

Danger lurks on the horizon, leaving only two choices: find shelter or flee. Cassidy Livingston's new identity has begun to feel as comfortable as her favorite sweater. She's been tucked away on Lantern Beach for weeks, waiting to testify against a deadly gang, and is settling in to a new life she wants to last forever. When she thinks she spots someone malevolent from her past, panic swells inside her. If an enemy has found her, Cassidy won't be the only one who's a target. Everyone she's come to love will also be at risk. Dangerous waters threaten to pull her into an overpowering chasm she may never escape. Can

Cassidy survive what lies ahead? Or has the tide fatally turned against her?

Perilous Riptide

Just when the current seems safer, an unseen danger emerges and threatens to destroy everything. When Cassidy Livingston finds a journal hidden deep in the recesses of her ice cream truck, her curiosity kicks into high gear. Islanders suspect that Elsa, the journal's owner, didn't die accidentally. Her final entry indicates their suspicions might be correct and that what Elsa observed on her final night may have led to her demise. Against the advice of Ty Chambers, her former Navy SEAL boyfriend, Cassidy taps into her detective skills and hunts for answers. But her search only leads to a skeletal body and trouble for both of them. As helplessness threatens to drown her, Cassidy is desperate to turn back time. Can Cassidy find what she needs to navigate the perilous situation? Or will the riptide surrounding her threaten everyone and everything Cassidy loves?

Deadly Undertow

The current's fatal pull is powerful, but so is one detective's will to live. When someone from Cassidy Livingston's past shows up on Lantern Beach and warns her of impending peril, opposing currents collide, threatening to drag her under. Running would be easy. But leaving would break her heart. Cassidy must decipher between the truth and lies, between reality and deception. Even more importantly, she must decide whom to trust and whom to fear. Her life depends on it. As danger rises and answers surface, everything Cassidy thought she knew is tested. In order to survive, Cassidy must take drastic measures and end the battle against the ruthless gang DH-7 once and for all. But if her final mission fails, the consequences will be as deadly as the raging undertow.

LANTERN BEACH ROMANTIC SUSPENSE

Tides of Deception

Change has come to Lantern Beach: a new police chief, a new season, and . . . a new romance? Austin Brooks has loved Skye Lavinia from the moment they met, but the walls she keeps around her seem impenetrable. Skye knows Austin is the best thing to ever happen to her. Yet she also knows that if he learns the truth about her past, he'd be a fool not to run. A chance encounter brings secrets bubbling to the surface, and danger soon follows. Are the life-threatening events plaguing them really accidents . . . or is someone trying to send a deadly message? With the tides on Lantern Beach come deception and lies. One question remains—who will be swept away as the water shifts? And will it bring the end for Austin and Skye, or merely the beginning?

Shadow of Intrigue

For her entire life, Lisa Garth has felt like a supporting character in the drama of life. The designation never bothered her—until now. Lantern Beach, where she's settled and runs a popular restaurant, has boarded up for the season. The slower pace leaves her with too much time alone. Braden Dillinger came to Lantern Beach to try to heal. The former Special Forces officer returned from battle with invisible scars and diminished hope. But his recovery is hampered by the fact that an unknown enemy is trying to kill him. From the moment Lisa and Braden meet, danger ignites around them, and both are drawn into a web of intrigue that turns their lives upside down. As shadows creep in, will Lisa and Braden be able to shine a light on the peril around them? Or will the encroaching darkness turn their worst nightmares into reality?

Storm of Doubt

A pastor who's lost faith in God. A romance

writer who's lost faith in love. A faceless man with a deadly obsession. Nothing has felt right in Pastor Jack Wilson's world since his wife died two years ago. He hoped coming to Lantern Beach might help soothe the ragged edges of his soul. Instead, he feels more alone than ever. Novelist Juliette Grace came to the island to hide away. Though her professional life has never been better, her personal life has imploded. Her husband left her and a stalker's threats have grown more and more dangerous. When Jack saves Juliette from an attack, he sees the terror in her gaze and knows he must protect her. But when danger strikes again, will Jack be able to keep her safe? Or will the approaching storm prove too strong to withstand?

LANTERN BEACH PD

On the Lookout

When Cassidy Chambers accepted the job as police chief on Lantern Beach, she knew the island had its secrets. But a suspicious death with potentially far-reaching implications will test all her skills —and threaten to reveal her true identity. Cassidy enlists the help of her husband, former Navy SEAL Ty Chambers. As they dig for answers, both uncover parts of their pasts that are best left buried. Not everything is as it seems, and they must figure out if their John Doe is connected to the secretive group that has moved onto the island. As facts materialize, danger on the island grows. Can Cassidy and Ty discover the truth about the shadowy crimes in their cozy community? Or has darkness permanently invaded their beloved Lantern Beach?

Attempt to Locate

A fun girls' night out turns into a nightmare when armed robbers barge into the store where Cassidy and her friends are shopping. As the situation escalates and the men escape, a massive manhunt launches on Lantern Beach to apprehend the dangerous trio. In the midst of the chaos, a potential foe asks for Cassidy's help. He needs to find his sister who fled from the secretive Gilead's Cove community on the island. But the more Cassidy learns about the seemingly untouchable group, the more her unease grows. The pressure to solve both cases continues to mount. But as the gravity of the situation rises, so does the danger. Cassidy is determined to protect the island and break up the cult . . . but doing so might cost her everything.

First Degree Murder

Police Chief Cassidy Chambers longs for a break

from the recent crimes plaguing Lantern Beach. She simply wants to enjoy her friends' upcoming wedding, to prepare for the busy tourist season about to slam the island, and to gather all the dirt she can on the suspicious community that's invaded the town. But trouble explodes on the island, sending residents—including Cassidy—into a squall of uneasiness. Cassidy may have more than one enemy plotting her demise, and the collateral damage seems unthinkable. As the temperature rises, so does the pressure to find answers. Someone is determined that Lantern Beach would be better off without their new police chief. And for Cassidy, one wrong move could mean certain death.

Dead on Arrival

With a highly charged local election consuming the community, Police Chief Cassidy Chambers braces herself for a challenging day of breaking up petty conflicts and tamping down high emotions. But when widespread food poisoning spreads among potential voters across the island, Cassidy smells something rotten in the air. As Cassidy examines every possibility to uncover what's going on, local enigma Anthony Gilead again comes on her radar. The man is running for mayor and his cult-like following is growing at an alarming rate. Cassidy feels certain he has a spy embedded in her inner circle. The problem is that her pool of suspects gets deeper every day. Can Cassidy get to the bottom of what's eating away at her peaceful island home? Will voters turn out despite the outbreak of illness plaguing their tranquil town? And the even bigger question: Has darkness come to stay on Lantern Beach?

<u>#7 Mucky Streak</u>

<u>#8 Foul Play</u>

<u>#9 Broom & Gloom</u>

<u>#10 Dust and Obey</u>

<u>#11 Thrill Squeaker</u>

<u>#11.5 Swept Away (novella)</u>

<u>#12 Cunning Attractions</u>

<u>#13 Cold Case: Clean Getaway</u>

<u>#14 Cold Case: Clean Sweep</u>

<u>While You Were Sweeping, A Riley Thomas Spinoff</u>

When Holly Anna Paladin is given a year to live, she embraces her final days doing what she loves most—random acts of kindness. But when one of her extreme good deeds goes horribly wrong, implicating Holly in a string of murders, Holly is suddenly in a different kind of fight for her life. She knows one thing for sure: she only has a short amount of time to make a difference. And if helping the people she cares about puts her in danger, it's a risk worth taking.

#1 Random Acts of Murder

#2 Random Acts of Deceit

#2.5 Random Acts of Scrooge

#3 Random Acts of Malice

THE WORST DETECTIVE EVER:

I'm not really a private detective. I just play one on TV.

Joey Darling, better known to the world as Raven Remington, detective extraordinaire, is trying to separate herself from her invincible alter ego. She played the spunky character for five years on the hit TV show *Relentless*, which catapulted her to fame and into the role of Hollywood's sweetheart. When her marriage falls apart, her finances dwindle to nothing, and her father disappears, Joey finds herself on the Outer Banks of North Carolina, trying to piece together her life away from the limelight. But as people continually mistake her for the character she played on TV, she's tasked with solving real life crimes . . . even though she's terrible at it.

#1 Ready to Fumble

#2 Reign of Error

#3 Safety in Blunders

#4 Join the Flub

#5 Blooper Freak

#6 Flaw Abiding Citizen

#7 Gaffe Out Loud

USA Today has called Christy Barritt's books "scary, funny, passionate, and quirky."

Christy writes both mystery and romantic suspense novels that are clean with underlying messages of faith. Her books have won the Daphne du Maurier Award for Excellence in Suspense and Mystery, have been twice nominated for the Romantic Times Reviewers' Choice Award, and have finaled for both a Carol Award and Foreword Magazine's Book of the Year.

She is married to her Prince Charming, a man who thinks she's hilarious—but only when she's not trying to be. Christy is a self-proclaimed klutz, an avid music lover who's known for spontaneously bursting into song, and a road trip aficionado.

When she's not working or spending time with her family, she enjoys singing, playing the guitar, and exploring small, unsuspecting towns where people have no idea how accident-prone she is.

Find Christy online at:
www.christybarritt.com
www.facebook.com/christybarritt
www.twitter.com/cbarritt

Sign up for Christy's newsletter to get information on all of her latest releases here: **www.christybarritt. com/newsletter-sign-up/**

If you enjoyed this book, please consider leaving a review.